the bedtime prince

Renée Tamsin

ISBN: 979-8-9852465-5-1

dedication

to those who came before me, and for the sake of
those who will come after

chapters

preface

I thrive on stories. They constantly surround me—in the books I read, the shows I watch, the music I listen to, even in my conversations. We all are. What makes humans so spectacular is that we live stories as well.

I believe in a force that binds families together—past present and future. Part of that binding is the connecting of stories. Everyone's story is a prologue to someone else's or an epilogue to someone who's come before.

My Oma's name was Hazel. Small, delicate but fierce woman who gracefully clung to old-fashioned values and standards.

My great-great uncle's name was Rolly. Jolly, energetic man with a goofy smile.

My great aunt's name was Linda. Sweet, beautiful woman with a deep smile that hangs in our family home.

My paternal grandma is a sufferer of chronic illness, but powers through with astounding strength.

My mom and my maternal grandma are selfless, gentle women who would do absolutely anything for their kids and grandkids.

My sister is an avid family historian who pours over records and journals and photos to piece together our genealogy.

My grandpa is an imaginative and ambitious man who never lets anyone tell him to dream smaller.

the bedtime prince is a complete fabrication.

None of the events you're about to read is true in any way. Names were used, personalities and vigor were borrowed, but the story is total fiction. Even so, it serves as a sort of ode to family history as a whole.

To my family history.

Parts of all of the traits and family members I've mentioned can be found in these pages, in various forms, and I hope I've done them justice.

So, here's to you.

INTERVIEW WITH HAZEL ALBRIGHT

AS RECORDED, TRANSCRIBED, AND EDITED BY KEIRA SAWYER ON APRIL 30, 2019

In following my mom's suggestion, I've charged my voice recorder and made an appointment with my Great Aunt Hazel. She was recently diagnosed with acute liver failure, so if there's any time to get her story recorded for posterity it's now, before she passes. The medications she's on have been affecting her mind—and if they aren't doing her much good, she probably doesn't have much time left. Mom and Dad visited her last week and noticed signs like hesitation and mixing up names; hopefully I can get a story or two from her before it's too late.

She promised me a plate of cookies with this visit, so that feels optimistic. If she forgets the stories, at least I still get cookies.

Before I go in, I might as well preface this with her basic information.

My father's aunt, Hazel Albright, was born in 1936, married in 1958, no kids. She worked as a teacher for a few decades before retirement. She must have done well for herself; her house is pretty nice and well-kept.

She's had hired help throughout the years, I think. I spoke with her home-care aide, Juliet, who's been with her for four years now.

"Hi, I'm—" I begin when she answers the door.

"Keira," she nods. She's a younger black woman—maybe four or five years older than I am—with a smirk on her face. I like her so far; she doesn't waste time. "Mrs. Albright said you were a redhead. She's in the living room, ready for you."

Juliet lets me in and leads me to Aunt Hazel. Hazel is sitting comfortably in her antique armchair. A vintage record player in the corner is playing some old French record I don't recognize, lulling Hazel into a distant reverie. She doesn't even stir when Juliet brings me to her, so I patiently sit on the couch nearest her, waiting until the song ends.

"Oh, Ellen," Hazel smiles at me.

"Keira," I gently correct.

Hazel smiles again and shakes her head. "Yes, that's what I meant. Ellen's daughter. You look just like her. Do you know this record? Lucienne Boyer. She was lovely...."

"Mrs. Albright," Juliet pats the old woman's arm and sets a plate of cookies on the small table between us. I mouth the words "thank you". I love Hazel, but the cookies were my big motivator. "Do you want me to get your photo album?"

Hazel's eyes light up. "Oh yes. Let me show you my photos, Keira." She takes the album and immediately opens it in the middle. Her smile is adorable, like a child. "That's my brother," she points at a picture of a middle-aged man in a wheelchair.

I know him. He's my Grandpa Rolly. He has a goofy smile on his face, which was no less than I would expect. He was a very light and bubbly man, full of jokes and smiles. He was everyone's favorite person, including Hazel's.

"Rolly's so sweet," Hazel goes on. "So happy. I wish I had that smile. And there—you know who that is?" She points at an older black woman standing behind grandpa's wheelchair. The way she waves Juliet over makes me nervous—please don't say "that's you" to the nearest black woman. Please.

To my surprise, Juliet chuckles. "Me, huh?" She rubs Hazel's shoulder and kisses the top of her head.

Hazel smiles and rolls her eyes. "Oh, you love to give me a hard time, don't you." She lowers her head as if telling me a secret. "I called her Miss Hollis once. Now I never hear the end of it. It's a compliment, you know," she calls to Juliet, who is now in the kitchen getting Hazel's medicine sorted and her tea brewed. "Miss Hollis was the tops. Funniest, wisest, greatest woman you could ever meet. Just like Jules. Did you know Juliet is going to become a doctor? Raised her own siblings and now she's going to change the world and heal hundreds of people." Juliet humbly waves off the compliment. "She worked for mama for years. She took care of Rolly and me as kids."

"Miss Hollis did?"

"Yes, of course, she did."

Jumping on her current train of thought, I aim my recorder a little closer and pose my first question.

"How long did she work for you?"

Hazel pauses for a moment, trying to recall. "I can't remember. A long time, though..." She flips through the album a little more and loses herself in the memories. Every couple of pictures, she points and smiles. I notice she's backtracking, looking through pictures from before her own birth. "Since Rolly was born, I think...it was just the three of them for a long time."

"When did you come in, Aunt Hazel? Where does your story start?"

Abruptly, she shuts the album. "My story isn't that interesting. I was born. I grew up. I lived part of a life that's now a fog. And now they tell me I have liver failure."

Her tone shifted, sharp and biting, which alarms me. I clear my throat a little, and Juliet must have heard me because within seconds she was back in the room and handing Hazel a cup of tea.

"Well, why don't you start with Rolly's story then?" she suggests to her. She rubs the old lady's arm again and takes a seat on the couch beside me. "You love talking about Rolly. Tell her that story Rolly used to tell you all the time."

This softens her back up. Hazel takes a cookie from the plate, which I've already been taking from, and munches on it with that grin returning to her face. "He was quite a storyteller, my Rolly. And he had an exciting childhood, you know."

I sigh impatiently, which thankfully only Juliet notices. I have a terrible poker face. Juliet is a great buffer, though. She reminds me of one of my older sisters. She doesn't take offense to my impatience and instead smiles at me, nodding in encouragement.

"Rolly's story is very important in understanding Hazel's," she promises.

"I guess that could be fun," I settle. I mean, I came for a story—why not take advantage and enjoy my grandpa's childhood? He died when I was in middle school.

Hazel finishes chewing and swallowing her cookie before returning to the conversation. "Fun," she repeats. "That was Rolly. He was quite a little chatterbox too. Nothing could slow him down—he probably told me the same story every night before bed. It was our bedtime tradition. His story and one of mama's cookies. He made everything better. I do miss him...."

"What story did he tell?" I press.

She smiles again, her eyes aimed past us. "It was the story of a princess named mama...."

the princess

Mama was never good with men. She liked them all well enough; she wanted to get married so badly. Rolly's dad died when he was a baby, so he never met him. It was always him and mama at the beginning. Mama hated it. Not Rolly—she loved Rolly always. It was the working and the providing and being both parents she hated. It's hard enough being a mama. Being a mama without the child's papa is even harder.

She barely saw Rolly during the day. Their time was in the evening when they ate Miss Hollis's dinner and talked before bedtime. Rolly never minded being alone with Miss Hollis and his schoolwork until then—Miss Hollis was like another mama.

Mama worked for a fancy businessman as his personal assistant. Not a secretary—a personal assistant. There was a difference, you know. Back then, women didn't work all that much and when they did, it was as maids or secretaries or what have you.

Oh, what did Rolly call him then...Russell Bellamy. Mr. Bellamy was her boss and he was one of the most successful tycoons in the area at the time. He was in real estate—buying, trading, leasing, merging; he did it all. Good at what he did. And there was always mama, sitting right beside him, taking notes and whispering suggestions. She knew her place but she always had the best ideas. And he actually listened to them.

She made good money, mama did. But you wouldn't know it, looking at Rolly. He had shoes and food and clothes, sure. But their house was small and dingy—I think they lived just outside of the slummy neighborhood. Rolly looked poor so he always played with the other poor children. Mama saved money. She knew what it was like to be poorer than dirt—she grew up that way, and then the Depression hit and made them even poorer. Rolly's papa left her with nothing, so she had to pick herself up, dust herself off, and get to work.

Miss Hollis always said mama was the best at that.

Picking herself up, dusting herself off, and getting back to work.

Mama hated working so she was always trying to get herself a husband. She said "a woman's place is with her babies and anything that keeps her from them just weighs her down." Things were different then. Especially for mama.

She tried real hard, though. The money she didn't save or use for Rolly's essentials, she used to make herself more desirable. If she could only nab a husband who could work and pay the bills, she could settle down and just be a mama. Men like that weren't as easy as you'd expect—especially the men she knew. Every time Mr. Bellamy had a dinner party or business conference, she'd gussy herself up all nice and pretty and be sure to smile at all the eligible businessmen. Rich men were ideal. I don't think that's ever changed. At least in my day it was still true. They have refined taste, though, so you do have to try a little harder.

the princess

I remember once my daddy told me she even bought herself a corset—when they came back in style, of course. She was always so stylish. Mr. Bellamy wanted his staff to be aesthetically pleasing and proper. Appearances were very important in this business. Mama being his assistant, and a very pretty lady herself, he made sure she wore nice clothes. Mama always thought she was still too curvy from when Rolly was born and no one pays much attention to you if they can tell you've had kids. Rolly was about....hm, how old was he....it was about 1934 so, he had to have been eight years old already. But she still thought her baby fat was just too much in her midsection. Mama was always a small lady, though. Low self-esteem and ridiculous expectations are age-old, sweetie. Never doubt that—every woman in history thought she was too fat or too skinny at some point in her life.

There was one particular dinner party; the one when she wore that corset right underneath her prettiest red dress—mama said ladies always look best in red. She poured the drinks (like she always did), she smiled (like she always did) and all the men loved to look at her (like they always did). But no marriage proposals.

The glances weren't any more than normal. The same three men, who had all rejected her in the past, smiled and looked but quickly moved on. For a woman as old-fashioned as mama, she was desperate for love and that makes you bold. She didn't get the response she wanted. She even flirted with one of them who was polite enough to carry on a conversation. High society is full of schmoozers, so this wasn't uncommon. Unfortunately, mama was too naive not to misread kindness.

But Mr. Bellamy noticed. He was a shrewd, observant man. When business was being discussed, his senses were like a hawk hunting its prey. No detail escaped him. That's what made him so successful. He spotted the details and then attacked when necessary. He took mama aside when the party changed rooms (Mr. Bellamy's house had a lot of big rooms for parties, so when dinner ended, there were at least two other rooms for sitting and chatting).

"Miss Sawyer," he whispered. "Why don't you head home? The business portion's over, the rest is just idle shop talk."

Confused, mama cleared her throat and adjusted that darn corset. "Are you sure, Mr. Bellamy? You won't be needing any notes taken?"

He caught her glimpse at the colleague of his she was targeting and he sighed. "He's not interested, Miss Sawyer. You look lovely, but he's only being polite. There's not much more you can do here. Go home, get some sleep—it's been a long day and you look exhausted. I'll see you in the morning."

Mr. Bellamy was a little harsh. He didn't pull punches in his personal or professional life. He kept a pretty assistant with him to soften the blows, I think. He was never one to be pushed around or deceived, which is great in business. But women need a gentler touch.

11

"Oh...um, yes, of course, sir...I'll...yes." Lucky for him, mama sighed too and just did what mama did best.

She picked herself up, dusted herself off, and got back to work.

But it's a process, honey. For everyone. And first she had to try and pick herself up.

It was a long workday and the evening Dinner of Disappointment was exhausting. She was tired, and it's always harder to pick yourself up when you're tired.

My husband pointed something out to me once: after a tough day, men put the day into boxes—one for work, one for family, one for fun, etc. But a woman has so many boxes that she has to use all at once so it's easier for them to spill. Some of us keep it nice and organized, but not when we're tired and hurt.

That night, mama went home with a spilling mind and a worn out body. She locked the door, tossed the corset on the bed, threw on a nightgown, and headed for her bed. It was too late to eat with Rolly—he was already in bed.

But Rolly never slept when mama was out. Never. The world wasn't right until mama walked through the door and sat by his bed. She was so beat that Rolly had to get up and remind her. She let out a sigh when she saw him at her bedroom door. It was a patient, motherly sigh—the kind they give when they know they love you but they wish you'd let them be.

"Mama, you're in time for a story," he told her, clinging to the door frame with excitement.

It was late, but he wasn't nearly tired enough to sleep. He had that goofy smile on his face, I'm sure—oh, I miss that goof.

Mama rubbed her face. She hadn't the energy to even pin her hair up and this boy wants her to tell a story. Her joints ached, alongside her heart, and she almost said no. But she's a good mama. And when you haven't seen your baby all day, you can't say the word "no".

"Okay, sweetheart," she sighed again. She wrapped her sore arms around his little shoulders and guided him to his bed. After tucking his anxious legs under their covers, she pressed her fingers against her temples, easing a headache she'd been nursing all day, and inhaled deeply. Mama's head and joints ached all the time for someone so young. They only slowed her down when her mind and heart were aching too.

"What kind of story do you want?" she asked him.

"What about your day? What did you do at work?" he sat up eagerly, ignoring mama's great job of tucking him in.

"You don't want to hear about that, Rolly. Trust me. It's incredibly boring and disappointing."

Rolly frowned. "Then you can just make it exciting, can't you? Mama, you can make anything sound exciting!"

"Um, alright. I'll tell you the story of a....princess."

"Are you the princess?"

"I don't know...I could be."

"I'll bet she was the prettiest in all the land."

"That's sweet, honey," she rubbed his cheek. "This princess was sad, though."

"Why was she sad?"

"Well...the princess went to a ball, where she hoped to meet a charming prince who could take her away and live happily ever after."

"Did the princess need saved from some villain? Great stories have a villain, mama."

"Of course, the princess was in great need of rescuing. She was being held captive by....uh....by a dragon."

"A terrifying dragon. That's good. I like dragons"

"Not this one. He was a great big dragon, with sharp pointed teeth, singeing fire breath, and complete disregard for the poor villagers and princess he held captive," she described.

"What does *disregard* mean?"

"He was cruel and rude and overworked them. They had to work late hours—"

"Like you do."

"Yes, like I do. He was a powerful dragon with a great big castle he lived in—it was the greatest castle in all the land. He made deals with kings and princes around him to keep the castle and get more gold and riches."

"Did any of his princes like the princess, like she wants?"

"No, sweetheart. No one liked the princess."

"That can't be true," Rolly shook his head.

"Not everyone likes your mama," mama told him. But little boys don't listen much.

"Maybe they just can't see you."

"Oh, they do, sweetheart. And that might be the problem."

Rolly's face fell. His mama's frown only deepened his. "So the ball wasn't a fun one. What happened?"

"The dragon kept her prisoner, like always, never to escape. He told the princess she looked tired and terrible and needed some sleep. So she went back to her room and went to bed." Mama leaned over and kissed Rolly on his head. "Just like you need to."

"Can we keep going tomorrow?" he asked.

"Of course, bug. Just no more tonight. Mama needs her sleep." She stood up from his bed and headed for her own.

"Goodnight mama. I hope you sleep good—you do look tired."

Mama sighed and went to bed. Men don't quite get it, do they?

Aunt Hazel pauses and snatches herself another cookie. It's a long pause, beyond the average mental break. Juliet and I look at each other and each take a cookie while we wait for her to continue.

"Did mama usually tell Rolly about her day?" I ask, gently guiding her back.

The old woman chuckles and waves a finger at me. "No, no. She never told him about work or Mr. Bellamy or anything. This was the first time. I think that's why it's his favorite story. He had such a clear memory of it too. Mama never liked talking about herself to anyone—I think she was afraid of people judging her. It was a different time then."

"She was tougher than nails, though, wasn't she?" Juliet prompts. "Tell Keira about what work was like."

"Oh, working in the castle guarded by the cruel dragon. Rolly loves the parts with the dragon." Hazel places the photo album back on her lap and opens to one of the early pages, pointing at one photo in particular.

The man looks familiar. He's handsome—dark hair, dark eyes, classy three-piece suit. He's probably in his mid-to-late thirties at the time the picture was taken. Everything about him screams "wealthy businessman." And, judging by his solemn expression and sharp features, I can understand why he's been described so harshly so far.

"The dragon," Hazel hums, ready to continue her tale.

the dragon

The dragon's castle was one of the oldest skyscrapers in the big city. It's a historic monument now, but it was relatively new at the time. The real estate business treated Bellamy well, but he was born into money. His family came from Ireland a generation before Russell and brought a lot of wealth with them. His father was a lawyer and his uncle was big in the Irish mob. Both became businessmen in their own right, but family is family. In those days it was hard not to overlap with mob dealings. They were everywhere.

But Russell Bellamy was even more straight-laced than his father. He ran a tight ship and didn't pay much mind to his cousin. He had a few buildings in the city, owned an opera house and several apartment buildings. He even built developments out in the smaller towns near the area.

The dragon's keep was a well-oiled machine, and it was all but run by mama. We're just such an organized gender, don't you think? Mama could take notes, remember all the important things, and make sure everyone else's jobs were done too. Women weren't managers then, but that's what mama did. They only *called* her a personal assistant.

Every morning Mr. Bellamy waltzed in, asked Mrs. Denning —his secretary—for his agenda for the day and would be handed a folder by mama. Mrs. Denning gave her the agenda the day before, she'd tell him.

He'd say, "Thank you, Miss Sawyer," without even looking at

them. He'd miss mama's wink at Mrs. Denning and he'd miss Mrs. Denning's grateful smile.

Mama took care of her people. Mrs. Denning was a terrible secretary. She could never figure out the phones, she always lost or forgot important papers, and she was a doormat. Lovely lady, though. I met her a few times. I think I even have a photo of her holding me as a baby. She loved mama for covering for her all the time. The poor lady was a widow—husband threw himself off a building—and she lost two of her children in a construction accident. She probably lost her mind to grief, but she kept it together enough of the time to help mama pretend she was good at her job.

"You're a lifesaver," she would tell her.

"I know," mama whispered back while she followed Bellamy into his office. She had gotten over the dinner party the night before. Mama was good at moving on. That was the *dusting herself off* part. And now she was getting back to work.

"Are you alright, honey?" Mrs. Denning reached for her arm to stop her before she went in. She was a concerned, middle-aged lady. Her dead son would've been mama's age so the poor lady projected all of her concern on mama.

Mama always looked tired, because she always was. Tired and sore. I never knew this until much later in life, but she was always sick, too. She had an upbeat energy when she was at work and sometimes when she came home, too. But it was all an act. Women are great pretenders. Well, most of us. I'm not that great at it. I suppose that's why I got a different set of problems than mama. She got what she could handle.

"As always," she answered. Every time. *Alright, as always.* That's never a good answer, but it was the only one she really gave. Mrs. Denning tightened her mouth, as she always did at that answer, and let her keep walking.

Mr. Bellamy had a lot of paperwork to catch up on— negotiating a merger or something like that. Boring man stuff, I suppose. Mr. Bellamy always had mama read over anything he worked on and signed because she was a better writer than he was. She could change something sharp like *it's my way or no way* to something diplomatic like *your input is appreciated, but we will be taking a different approach.*

They'd take hours to pour over a single contract, making it diplomatic, but airtight. He'd treat her to lunch, but only so they could continue the proofreading and scripting through their lunch break. He was a bit of a slave driver. For what it's worth, Rolly mentioned Bellamy always took mama wherever she wanted to eat. Sometimes it was somewhere fancy and high-end, and sometimes it was a small deli. He never cared (or noticed) what she ordered, so on days Miss Hollis would go home early from the house, she'd order a little extra to bring home for Rolly's dinner.

Then she and Mr. Bellamy would eat, gather up the

paperwork, and head back to the office to pick up where they left off. This particular day in Rolly's story, mama worked late. She worked late often, dictating memos and filing the day's work, but this time he kept her much later than dinner.

He never made anyone in his company work later or more strenuous hours than he wasn't willing to work himself. And his whole life was his work, so there was no time for funny business or laziness here. He flipped on his phonograph to keep mama occupied, while he read over the merger contract, or whatever nonsense was on his desk, once again. The problem was, Bellamy listened to classical music, which put mama to sleep.

"Do you have any other records, sir?" mama prodded.

He glanced up from his work with sharp eyes. "Do you have something against classical music, Miss Sawyer?"

She cleared her throat and shook her head. "No, of course not. It's very...soothing."

His eyes went back to the paperwork. "If you pour me a drink, you're welcome to change it," he offered.

Too eagerly, mama walked over to the phonograph and sifted through his shelf of vinyls. Her eagerness faded quickly—he had nothing but classical. Seeing her visible disappointment, Mr. Bellamy almost smiled.

"What would you prefer?" he asked. When she glanced back at him, his eyes were aimed at the papers again.

"Oh, I don't know. Maybe some Ray Noble? Lucienne Boyer? Something more..."

"Modern?"

"Well, yes," she chuckled. She reached for the decanter on the table adjacent, surrendering all hope of an uplifting track. She poured Bellamy a drink and set it next to his sprawled folders.

"Hm," was all he said.

Assuming her previous position in the neighboring chair, she rested her tired hand on the pad of paper now filled with his comments and amendments for the contract at hand. The orchestra droned on while she watched him occasionally twitch or grunt at lines he told her to correct.

She angled her face away while he dictated, so he couldn't see her mouth sour and her eyes droop as the next hour or so passed. Heavy steps outside of Bellamy's door jerked her awake.

Without knocking, this large, rough-looking man in a well-tailored suit barged into the office. Rolly always described him as a "fatter dragon." The suit suggested he had castles of his own, but he didn't carry himself in the classy way Mr. Bellamy did. Everyone knew who he was back then. Jimmy O'Shea. Second-generation Irish mob boss. Ruled a good number of the neighborhoods in the area at the time.

"I have a secretary for a reason," Mr. Bellamy told him, without looking up from his paperwork. He recognized the heavy step and rude entrance.

"She wasn't there," the fatter dragon gestured.

This time, Bellamy looked up, but not at the visitor—his eyes narrowed on mama. "Not there?"

"I sent her home," mama explained. As she did whenever a man entered the room, she sat up straighter and adjusted her dress. "It seemed a little late for her to be needed."

Bellamy nodded slowly, as if not realizing just how late it was. He shut the folder in front of him and rose from his chair. "What do you want, Jimmy? I'm busy."

O'Shea smiled one of those skeevy thug smiles. You know the type—where his eyes curl up just like his mouth. "I can see that," he replied. "She is a pretty one, isn't she?"

Mama blushed; adjusting her dress apparently worked. But she caught the wrong man's eye. Which is how it always goes—mama was never good with men. Her standards for good-looking men weren't the greatest either. O'Shea wasn't the most pleasant to look at. I don't have his picture, but I'm sure you can find one yourself. Gotta be somewhere on those computers.

She didn't appreciate this one bit, but Mr. Bellamy stepped out from behind his desk and stood in between mama and the mobster, obstructing the view.

"That's all for tonight, Miss Sawyer," he told her. He lifted her from her seat, to move her along quickly. "Go home and get some rest. We'll pick up again tomorrow."

"Do you want me to mail these—" she tried to linger.

"It can wait until tomorrow," he snapped. He didn't give her a chance to attempt another conversation toward the mobster. He put a hand to her back and gently pushed until she was through the office door. "Just go home. You look tired. Get some rest and I'll see you in the morning."

"Mr. Bellamy?"

"Yes?" he paused just a moment as he reached to close the door behind her.

She hesitated. He didn't often look directly into her eyes, but when he did she had a hard time looking away. "Um, should you be meeting with a man like Mr. O'Shea...alone?"

"So you know what kind of man he is, then." It wasn't a question. It was a confirming statement. Mama should know better than to flirt with a criminal. "You should be getting home, Miss Sawyer." Bellamy gave her a scolding eyebrow raise and closed the door, just as mama heard O'Shea exclaim,

"It's about time we talk. If I didn't know better, I'd think you're avoiding me. Never avoid family, sport."

It was usually late by the time she clocked out, and no woman should walk through New York City alone in the dark. No one really should, but especially a pretty young thing like mama. So she'd hail a cab, take it to the edge of her neighborhood, tip him well, and walk the rest of the way. When she got home that night, some of the neighborhood kids were still playing baseball under the street lights.

Kids did things like that back then. They played outside, late into the evening until their mamas called them home for dinner. And then, sometimes, they'd head back out after dinner and stay out until dark.

Miss Hollis was behind on laundry so she was hard at work while Rolly ran out to play a game or two before bed. He was never good at baseball—the poor kid had no coordination. But, boy, did he love the game. They always put him in the outfield. And I mean, as far into the outfield as he could be. He'd holler and cheer on everyone who came to bat. He never got a chance to swing a bat or even throw a ball, but being a part of the game was all he wanted. He never complained.

But mama did.

She knew how cruel kids could be, even if he didn't see it. He came by his naïveté honestly. But his part in the game wasn't her biggest complaint that night. It was later than any adult should've been out, but her eight year-old boy and the other kids were still out playing ball.

"Rolly, get over here!" she called to him, standing at the door to their apartment.

One of the other boys' moms opened her window and called back to mama. "It's okay, Miss Sawyer. I told him it was alright."

Mama inhaled bravely, as she did when facing the judging neighbors. "With all due respect, Mrs. Gallo, I'd rather Rolland not play outside after dark. Especially when he's too far for Miss Hollis to see from the window."

Mrs. Gallo pursed her lips. "I thought I'd give her a break. Being a mother and a maid is such tiring work, ya know."

Mama got comments like these all the time. Hers was the only home to afford hired help of any kind. Miss Hollis practically lived there. All of her children were grown, and her husband died in the war, so mama and Rolly were her whole life. Mama gave her work when she couldn't find any. Mr. Bellamy paid her well enough to afford good childcare, and Miss Hollis was the best. But mama was saving, so their neighbors at the time thought she was nothing more than a complicated snob who hated being with her child.

I remember Rolly telling me once that one of the other moms in the neighborhood thought he was an orphan because his mama was never home. When he told mama, she just smiled and kissed his head. He couldn't see her cry about it if she kissed the top of his head. Hiding your own pain from your babies is a hard thing, but mama did it.

She picked herself up, dusted herself off, and called her baby back home. Rolly always listened the first time she called. He was a good boy. Always was. He never had a rough age, like most boys. His mama was his hero, and he always listened to heroes.

"You're late, mama," he told her while she wiped the dirt off his face. "Does the dragon not like to sleep?"

"Dragons don't need sleep—they're too busy blowing fire up everyone's rear-ends," Hollis poked her head into the bathroom, where mama had Rolly up on the counter so she could reach his face without bending over. "I'm sorry, Miss Linda. Time passed right on by me. I wouldn't a-let him out so late if I saw how dark it was."

Mama just shrugged. "It's alright. I shouldn't have been there so late."

"Nah, miss, you gotta earn a livin' wage, don't ya?" Miss Hollis took the damp rag from mama's hand and wiped Rolly's face herself. "I'll get him ready for bed. You get yourself into a nightgown and relax."

Mama didn't have to be told twice. She stepped aside and went to her room to try and relax. Rolly made goofy faces while Miss Hollis kept on wiping them away.

"Why isn't mama wiping me?" Rolly asked her.

Miss Hollis shushed him and wiped a little more, until all the dirt was gone. "Mama's not well, baby. Sometimes she needs a rest."

"Why doesn't mama stay home from work and sleep all day long? Then she'd be better. That's what I do when I'm sick."

Things are so much simpler when you're a kid.

Miss Hollis chuckled. "It works for you, doesn't it. But when sick is your everyday, you don't feel it's fair to use it as an excuse, even if it's a good one. So mama just keeps going instead."

Rolly sat quiet for a minute while Hollis rinsed the dirty rag of all his face dirt. He wasn't usually quiet, but digesting important parts of stories requires silence sometimes.

"My mama's pretty strong," he declared.

Miss Hollis turned and grinned at him. "That's right, she is. She's gotta be to keep up with you, child." She took him down from the counter and gave him a swift pat on the back, launching him in the direction of his bedroom. "Now get yourself to bed—and if you're lucky, your mama may just have enough in her to continue that bedtime story."

"Tell me more about the dragon, mama. Did he have a lot of gold?"

Mama laid next to Rolly in the bed, stroking his head and subtly picking all the leftover baseball fun out of his hair. She didn't like talking about the dragon, but Rolly had a way of getting what he wanted. So mama rolled her eyes and humored him.

"Of course he did," she told him. "Remember, he has the biggest castle in all the land."

Rolly shook his head, moving mama's hand out of the way. "No, I mean, in a secret treasure cave. Maybe that's why he's so cruel.

He's protecting his secret treasure trove filled with gold and gems."

Mama considered this. "You know," she said. "I do believe he does. Every dragon probably does. The kingdoms they live in didn't let people have gold of their own. Only coins and paper."

Rolly giggled. "That seems stupid."

"Don't say stupid," mama chided, but then chuckled. "It is stupid, though, isn't it? That's why the dragons keep the gold such a secret."

That's true, actually. Just a little history lesson here, Keira. Did you know that when FDR took us off of the gold standard, he actually made it illegal to own gold bars? Made sense to a lot of people at the time—got us out of the Depression, maybe. But rich men don't always agree with the politicians they help fund. Bellamy, and others like him, were doing their part to help the poor without the suits in the big house stepping in. Given time, they probably could've banded together and done even more. Mobsters helped sometimes too—Al Capone even funded a soup kitchen. Funny, isn't it?

But you make it illegal to be wealthy in your own right and suddenly the wealthy get stingy again. Bellamy still helped out—he was a dragon, not a monster—but like every other dragon, he kept his contraband. Like booze in Prohibition. A vault of gold bars was the new speakeasy, and mama was right—just about every dragon had one.

"Did the princess know about the secret treasure?" he asked mama.

"She had a pretty good idea. But she didn't care."

"Why not? Gold and jewels and rich stuff, mama. Everybody cares about that. You could buy the nicest baseball bats and the juiciest hot dogs." He was making himself hungry.

"The princess didn't care about all that. She had all the riches she needed."

"Then what did she need?"

"She needed to be saved from the dragon. She needed to be loved."

Rolly frowned. "What kind of love did the princess need?"

Mama was too quiet for too long, so Rolly sat up and looked at her strangely until she answered him. "The kind of love...that doesn't leave when things get hard. The kind that's strong and safe and never fades away."

"I love you like that, mama."

Mama smiled the easiest smile she ever felt on her face. "Yes, you do. And I'll always love you like that too."

"Do you need a break?" Juliet asks her.

Hazel's eyes are welling with tears as she remembers Linda and Grandpa Rolly.

"The poor girl wanted love," she stares off blankly, ignoring Juliet's question. Her hand lightly taps the photo album on her lap. "Rolly's daddy didn't just die...."

Juliet goes to her side and touches her arm. "Mrs. Albright, do you want to rest a moment before we go on."

Almost jolting out of her train of thought, Aunt Hazel looked at Juliet in confusion. "Um...what was that, dear?"

"We can take a break," I offered. "Let's eat some lunch. We can get back to Rolly in a little bit."

Hazel nodded slowly and then quickly stood from her chair. "Yes, let's eat something. I need to rest for a minute before I get to the next part."

I'm glad I didn't turn off the recorder when we broke to eat—Aunt Hazel keeps going, thinking our break was over before it really began.

the dragon

the prince

The Depression hit everyone. No one really had it easy. So many lost their jobs and money when the stock market crashed, and a lot of them decided to end it all. Rolly's dad never would've killed himself on purpose. But he decided to end the life he was living by leaving mama, and that was even before the stock market crashed. He lost his job and couldn't support a family anymore, you see, and instead of working through it with mama and helping her raise Rolly, he walked out. Hit the railroad for a job that took him far away from the city.

The death came later.

Rolly said it was some kind of train accident. Mama never talked about it. I think she still hated him. She told everyone she was a widow—which was true. It wasn't as common to get divorced in those days, so they were still technically married, I supposed.

Mama was strong, but she didn't think she was.

That's why she met Calvin.

Calvin Priestley was a charming, handsome smooth-talker. He liked pretty women who took care of him. And my mama took care of people. He called her his sweetheart, she'd light up and buy him dinner. He told her he loved her and she paid for his hotel room. He never stayed anywhere more than a week or two—he wasn't the settling down type. Even with mama, he'd be around for a while and then gone for months.

Until a few days after mama told Rolly about the dragon's

gold.

Rolly played baseball with the other kids at a park a few blocks away when he saw Calvin walking down the street. He was far enough in the outfield to see him—Calvin was probably a ball's throw away—one of the better player's throws; Rolly couldn't throw worth beans.

Before he could call him over, he saw Calvin cross the street and talk to some guy Rolly had never seen before. My brother got around the neighborhood a lot, not having mama at home all day— and Miss Hollis trusted that he had a good head on his shoulders. He knew most of the faces in the area, even if he never spoke to them before.

This man didn't have a lot of distinguishing features, Rolly said, but he did remember him having a shaved head. That could be anyone, though. I've always thought bald men all look the same. Calvin seemed to be friends with him, whoever he was. They were whispering to each other, real low. When Rolly hollered Calvin's name, they both snapped up, and hushed their whispers.

"Cal!" Rolly shouted across the street, waving his arms like a maniac. "Calvin, come here!"

After shaking the bald man's hand, Calvin walked across to talk to Rolly, with a big smile on his face. He had a goofy one like Rolly did. Really pulls you in and makes you comfortable. He and Rolly were the best of friends. Calvin gave him his first baseball mitt;

Rolly talked about that for years, even though we all knew mama
gave him the money to buy it.

"You're back in town," Rolly grinned when Cal ruffled his
hair like a pal. "Are you coming to eat with us?"

Calvin crouched to Rolly's level—which wasn't too low, since
Calvin wasn't all that tall to begin with. "I'm surprising your mom
today. I'm gonna treat you both to the tastiest meal you can think of."

"Pretzels and hot dogs?" the boy hoped.

Calvin chuckled. "Maybe something your mama would like
too. Maybe a steak or something. I can take you to the stadium
another day, buddy."

"Man, did you find a lot of money somewhere, or what?"

"I found some, yeah. Where's your mom?"

"Well, she's at work. I'd take you there, but my team is
counting on me, so I can't leave the game just yet."

"That's okay, pal. She still work for Bellamy?" he slipped his
hands in his pockets.

"The dragon with all the gold," Rolly said in a goofy, spooky
voice. He then cracked a smile and giggled at his own joke. "Yeah, she
does. She's there all the time."

"Well, maybe I'll just surprise her there, then."

"Tell mama I said hi!"

"Okay. Good luck with the...outfield."

Rolly grinned and waved his mitt like a pro as Calvin walked away.

I never told you how mama got the job...

Oh, what did Rolly say mama used to be....a waitress or a teller or a maid or something. She was in someone's house, so perhaps she was a maid. Anyway, Bellamy met her at a business dinner at some rich man's house. Mama worked there with a couple of other girls. She hated it. Cleaning someone else's house and taking care of someone else's kid while she could barely afford to take care of her own. But she was always a hard worker, and she helped the other girls when they fell short.

Mr. Bellamy took notice, apparently, and was impressed with how well she juggled multiple duties at once. So he made her an offer and snatched her right out from under that other guy's nose.

Personal assistants make so much more than maids. At least his did. He worked them so hard in the past that he had a hard time keeping them. Mama lasted the longest. Around this time, she had been working for him for about three years—she started just a couple of years after Rolly's daddy died. Yes, that sounds right. In all that time, she never talked about her personal life. Goodness, Mr. Bellamy didn't even know Rolland existed. She didn't want to ruin the best job she knew she could get; a man like Mr. Bellamy didn't care what you went home to, just so long as you showed up on time and put in a good day's work.

So you can imagine the look on mama's face when Calvin Priestley walked into the office.

"What are you doing here?" mama's voice shook a little with nerves when he kissed her.

"I wanted to surprise you," he told her in a soft tone. "Aren't you surprised?"

Mama nodded a few times, glancing at Mrs. Denning's encouraging expression before answering. "So, so surprised. Did you go by the house yet, or did you just—"

"I missed you, so I wanted to pop in and treat you to lunch. Hi, I'm Calvin," he held a hand out for Mrs. Denning to shake.

"Mrs. Denning."

"Pleasure meeting another fine young lady," he winked at her.

Mrs. Denning giggled and blushed, playfully batting him away. "Oh Linda, you've got yourself a charmer here."

Mama didn't know what to say. She knew she had a charmer —that's why she liked him. So she gently massaged her hands, as she always did when she was suddenly stressed.

"How long have you been working with my girl here?" he sat on the corner of Mrs. Denning's desk.

"Your girl?" mama repeated, dazed.

"Oh, about a year," Mrs. Denning answered.

"And ya like it?" he asked.

"Linda's fantastic—but I'm not telling you anything you don't already know."

Calvin grabbed mama's hand and kissed it. "She's something else, isn't she?"

Mama smiled and relaxed her shoulders; this is what she liked to hear. She was almost forgiving the surprise visit she didn't ask for, until Mr. Bellamy's office door opened.

"Miss Sawyer, I need...."

Mr. Bellamy stood in the doorway for a moment, giving the visitor the once over. Men do this thing when they meet each other for the first time where they square their shoulders and jut out their chins just a little bit. Even men like Bellamy. He and Calvin jutted those chins until Calvin finally stepped forward, offering a hand.

"Mr. Bellamy, it's a pleasure to meet you."

Bellamy lifted his chin a little more, looking down his nose at the charmer. "And who might you be?"

"Calvin Priestley, sir. I'm Linda's beau."

"He was just stopping by, Mr. Bellamy," mama quickly chimed in. She was almost embarrassed. She always wanted men's attention, just never knew what to do with it once she got it. And Calvin's was so inconsistent and fleeting that he'd avoid words like *beau* and *going steady* like the plague.

"Ah, I see," Bellamy nodded. He stepped past Calvin and handed mama a folder. "We have a few more things to go over before

39

the meeting tonight."

Mama took the folder and lowered her voice in Calvin's direction. "I can't go to lunch, Cal—I'm working."

Bellamy signed something on Mrs. Denning's desk and turned back to continue work in his office. But Calvin wasn't happy with that, and he didn't like to be ignored. "Better not be keeping her through dinner too or you may have a protester on your hands, Mr. Bellamy."

Squaring his shoulders again, Mr. Bellamy smirked. "Nothing I haven't dealt with before. The meeting tonight is important; she'll be staying."

"All work, no play kinda fella, huh?"

"Cal," mama stopped him. "Why don't you just....meet me later?"

Calvin bit back his next retort. Instead, he nodded to Mr. Bellamy, said a polite little "good day to you, sir," and left the building to head for mama's house.

When Cal was around the corner and down the staircase, Mr. Bellamy pulled mama into his office with a confusing expression. She couldn't tell if he was cross with her—she could usually tell because he'd inhale real slow and tighten his jaw. That's how he always looked when he was upset. He was never one for shouting or throwing—just inhaling and tightening that jaw of his.

"I'm so sorry, sir. I didn't expect him to show up

unannounced like that. I would have never—"

"It's alright, Miss Sawyer," Bellamy assured her. Then he said something mama never would've expected. "You can leave early tonight."

Mama almost got hit by the door as he closed it behind them. She was so shocked. "Um...are you sure?"

"Something tells me Mr. Priestley doesn't often treat a woman like yourself to dinner. Shouldn't let an opportunity like that go to waste."

"Thank you, sir," she smiled.

But then his brow wrinkled while he took the folder from mama again and sorted through it himself.

"Are you sure it's alright? The meeting's important, and I'd understand if you need me."

Realizing the face he was making, he looked up and put on a smile. "It's not a problem, Miss Sawyer. He just wasn't what I would've imagined."

Mama was used to defending her decisions. Calvin was a decision she defended on a regular basis. To everyone too—Miss Hollis, the neighbors—everyone with good sense about them. She hoped she'd never have to defend him to Mr. Bellamy, but Calvin had to go on and spoil things.

"He's a good man," she claimed.

"I'm sure he is."

"He doesn't usually do things like that; he must have something important planned," she commented.

"And that's what you've wanted," he pointed out.

"Well, I won't be beautiful forever, sir. I'm hardly beautiful now. My chances aren't very promising, are they?"

"Hm. Yes, well, we should get this looked over before I bring it to the board this afternoon."

She didn't expect Mr. Bellamy to tell her she was beautiful—she told Rolly that she never thought he saw much past the end of his nose unless it was a black-and-white contract or dollar bills. Even so, it would've been nice if he had at least complimented her dress every once in a while. He did pay for it, after all.

When mama got home that night, Rolly and Calvin were playing with Rolly's new toy. Calvin liked to spoil him whenever he came to town, and a boy as happy and lovely as Rolly was thrilled with any old thing. But this time, Cal got him a Buck Rogers ray gun. Every boy wanted one. They weren't all that great—Rolly kept his for years and I never thought much of it. It was from Cal, and Cal was his hero. More importantly, it made Rolly feel like a hero himself. He showed him how to aim and told him which parts of the imaginary bad guy to shoot in order to win.

Sounds like a boy's dream come true, but it wasn't my mama's. Coming home was hard enough after a long day, but it was even harder when Cal sent Miss Hollis home early. He said she looked tired and needed a rest, so he was doing her a favor. Mama understood that—housework all day was just as exhausting as running around an office. What mama didn't understand was why the dinner table was empty. No trace of that meal he was supposedly treating her to. It was getting late and Rolly would be needing to go to bed within the next hour or two. But Calvin was "keeping Rolly busy" in the living room with the toy gun, so mama put her bag in her room and tried to cook dinner.

Mama's mama died when she was a young girl, and her grandma was too impatient to teach a child how to make a full-course meal. Mama could make a good sandwich or soup, but that was about it. Rolly loved her sandwiches, and they were the easiest, so she set to preparing them while Calvin laid on the couch watching Rolly shoot his toy gun into the air.

"Should we help mama?" Rolly considered for a moment.

"Nah, she makes good sandwiches on her own," Cal told him. He waved a lazy hand and then made a picture frame with his fingers in the direction of the grandfather clock across the room. "Bet you can't hit the top of that," he challenged.

Never challenge Rolly. The boy could never say no. To anything. I once got him to drink half a bottle of Tabasco sauce, just by telling him he couldn't do it. He liked pushing himself. The lovable nut.

43

So Rolly aimed that dumb gun with the imaginary bullets at the top of the grandfather clock.

"Pretend it's the biggest bad guy around," Cal suggested.

"Like the dragon with the hidden gold," Rolly seethed in that deep voice he did whenever he played a tough guy. He pulled the trigger and imagined a perfect shot, cheering in victory. Then he snapped his head toward Cal. "What does he look like?"

"What does who look like?"

"The dragon."

"Ooh, I'd imagine he has big shiny scales all over, sharp teeth to chomp your head off, and maybe—"

"No, no—the *dragon*! Mama said you met him today."

Calvin slowly sat up on the couch, staring at Rolly curiously. "You mean Bellamy?"

"Yeah, him. What's he look like?"

"Why's he the dragon?"

"Because he's mean to the princess. He keeps her captive, you know. In his castle. Which is probably where he keeps all his gold hidden."

Cal lifted an eyebrow. "Where'd he get all the gold?"

"He stashed it away when the kingdom wouldn't let him keep it. Can you imagine that? They wouldn't let him have his own gold. So it's a secret treasure he has hidden away. That's why he's so crabby all the time and keeps the princess locked up."

44

"Well that's not very fair for the princess, is it?"

Rolly shook his head. "It certainly is not."

Mama called the boys into the kitchen for sandwiches, and the conversation was over. Rolly didn't learn what the dragon looked like until much later. But he was alright with that—right now he had Calvin and his new toy. After dinner, dishes, and after Calvin neglected to propose to mama and went to his hotel instead (with a check from mama to pay for the week, of course), Rolly prepared himself for more of his little story.

Mama rubbed her eyes and sighed. "Where did I leave off last time?"

Rolly knelt on his bed with his hands on his knees, excited without even a sliver of the exhaustion my mama always felt that time of night. "Hmm...the dragon had the princess. Can you have someone fight the dragon? There needs to be a hero. There's always a hero."

Nodding, mama rested her head against Rolly's headboard. "Yes, you're right. There is always a hero. This story has a hero too. He's a strong, handsome prince—"

"And he saves the princess."

"Well," mama shifted. "He promises to, sure."

"So he'll fight the dragon, save the princess, and take her away from the evil dragon's castle," Rolly settled back, confident in his narrative.

Mama smiled; it was a tired smile, not a deep smile. Rolly told me she didn't have a deep smile for a long time. Actually, he never saw mama's deep smile until he was closer to nine years old. She was so tired, so unhappy. I'm glad I never met that mama. I would've loved her all the same, but the memories wouldn't have been so sweet.

Rolly disagreed. He'd keep telling me I was wrong and that mama's tired smile meant the world to him because she made it just for him. When she was wiped out, with a broken heart and a broken body, she pushed herself to give that tired smile, and Rolly soared. The mama I knew smiled all the time. Deep smiles. The kind that gives you wrinkles, and makes it hard for other people to frown at you. Mama had the greatest smile. Stretched across her whole face until it lit up her eyes. But that's what makes Rolly's story more interesting I suppose. It's the story of how mama got her deep smile.

I pause the recorder and let her take a quick nap. When she returns, she herself is wearing a "deep smile" and practically skipping into the room.

"Did I tell you about his dog?" she asks.

I shake my head and Juliet says, "I don't even think you've told me *about Rolly's dog. What was his name?"*

"Oh, she was a little girl dog, but he didn't know that when he found her."

"Found her, huh? Was she a stray?" I ask.

Hazel just chuckles and sits back in her armchair.

the prince

the noble steed

Rolly never liked school much. He was too hyperactive.
Always chatting in the back of the classroom. He loved people—he
didn't love numbers and letters and memorizing the order they
should be in. And with mama working so much, and Miss Hollis
running errands and doing their housework, Rolly would often walk
toward the school, find himself distracted, and then wander off on an
adventure for the day. He'd realize the time when he got hungry for
lunch, and then he'd head home.

Back then, they didn't care too much about kids in school.
They'd be lucky if kids ate, so no one was out hunting down truants if
they didn't show up to class. Rolly once went weeks before going
back to school.

Well, his skipping class was even worse when Calvin was in
town. Calvin was fun, you see. That's all he did. He had fun and he
made money, somehow. Taking Rolly along on his adventures was a
given. It kept his connection with mama, I suppose. Watching her kid
gave him an implied invitation to dinner, then his charm and smile
kept the door open.

One day, Calvin and Rolly were strolling around, avoiding
school and telling stories. Calvin asked him more about that dragon
and his gold and Rolly just loved making things up. Cal only half-
listened, I'm sure. He always had other things on his mind anyway.
They walked a bit until Rolly saw a little brownish grey dog digging
through the trash.

Papa said she was probably part Schnauzer but we never bothered finding out and Rolly never cared. Heck, he didn't even care what gender she was—he just saw a dog and decided it was his new best friend. Thought it was a little boy dog for the longest time. He named her Murphy and everything.

He stopped his story mid-sentence and ran over to pet her. Cal would've kept on walking if he hadn't noticed the sudden halt in chatter. When he made it back to Rolly, the boy had already named the mutt and decided to help it hunt for food.

"You think your mama's gonna let you bring that thing into the house?" Cal posed.

Rolly put his hands on his hips proudly. "And why not? Every soldier needs a noble steed. Mama knows that—she knows all about heroes. She'll let me. We just need to get him some food."

Somehow he talked Cal into walking down the street to buy the dog a treat. But there were conditions—there were always conditions with that man. Cal gave Murphy a small treat, and bought one for Rolly while he was at it, keeping the boy and the dog distracted. They kept up on their walk until they were in a slummy neighborhood, miles from Rolly's house. The boy hardly noticed. He just munched on his biscuit and tuned out whatever instructions Cal gave him.

It was just as well. Rolly and Murphy were too busy fighting dragons with his toy gun to notice where Cal slunk off to. They ran and hid and ran again. Rolly spun around quick, kicked the air a few times, and even tried to ride Murphy at some point. She was too small a dog for him to fit, but she was his noble steed nonetheless. In his eyes, she was a large stallion with a majestic mane, war-worn legs, but a fighter's spirit.

Just when they were closing in on the dragon's henchmen in the forest, Rolly noticed Calvin had disappeared. It was just him and Murphy in the middle of an unfamiliar neighborhood.

"Where could he have gone so fast?" he asked Murphy. Not that she would respond, but he pretended she shrugged in mutual confusion.

They were just outside a shanty-looking apartment building, but there were no kids playing, like in his neighborhood. He wasn't sure if he should find a grownup and ask for directions home, or if he and Murphy should just start this new quest alone. He was a confident kid, so the decision was actually pretty simple. As long as he wandered home by nightfall, he was okay. So he gave Murphy the best pep talk anyone could give a loyal animal companion before a battle—shame no one was there actually listening to him. He couldn't even remember what he said when he told me this part. But I'm sure it was inspiring.

In any case, before they set off for home without Calvin, a young police officer came running out from the nearest apartment building. His hair was wild from distress; he huffed and puffed, like he had just run down two flights of stairs.

"Hey kid!" he shouted at Rolly. Rolly thought he was in trouble—because he usually was—so he froze and stood in front of Murphy, just in case the officer planned to take away his new friend.

"Oh, h-hi," Rolly stuttered. He did that when he was nervous. Words escaped him, even though his brain moved faster than his little legs ever could.

The officer wasn't scolding him, though. Once he caught his breath, he asked, "Are you afraid of heights?"

Rolly wasn't afraid of many things. And climbing a tall height was just what he planned to do when scaling a tree to ambush the dragon's henchmen anyway. He could use the practice. "Oh no, sir. I'm not afraid of anything," he lied.

He was afraid of water, oddly enough. Never stepped foot in a swimming pool or a lake or an ocean in his life. He took short baths and never put his face under water. I never understood why, and he never had a good reason. Even so, he only half-lied—water was all there was. He wasn't afraid of much else.

The officer grabbed his hand and led him into the apartment building, Murphy following loyally behind them. Probably a dozen people were gathered in the hall, around this one door, waiting for the officer to return. The door was locked, and for some reason, all of them wanted to see what was on the other side.

"I'm gonna lift you up to this window." The officer pointed to the transom window above the door. It was up high, and just big enough for a small boy like Rolly to wiggle through. "And I'll need you to crawl through and open the door from the inside.

Rolly was up for anything. He let the officer lift him onto his shoulders until he could reach the transom with his hands. With impressive strength, he pulled himself through the window and landed (almost) on his feet on the other side of the door. He twisted his ankle a bit with the landing, but nothing he couldn't handle. Obediently, he unlocked the door and let the officer and the small hoard of people into the apartment. Poor boy didn't even notice what was inside until his eyes followed the officer to the dead body on the ground.

The poor man who lived there was lying on the ground, in the middle of the room, with three bullet wounds. Papa showed me the news article they wrote about Theodore Finch, but only when I was old enough to understand what Rolly was actually looking at. Murder wasn't something every child really understands. Even Rolly didn't really understand. He saw blood, but he didn't think the man was dead. He just assumed the officer was going to help the man now, so he could leave with Murphy and head home.

That wasn't the case.

The man who lived there was killed somehow and left in the apartment, which was locked on the inside. It stumped the police, and was never solved. I always thought the killer could've been hiding in the apartment still, and then snuck out when Rolly opened the door and all the people came in. Or he killed him in the hallway so when Mr. Finch backed into his apartment, he locked the door and then fell down dead.

It looked a lot more clever than it probably was. I don't know; I think papa knew who did it but he never talked about it. Mama knew who did it too, but neither of them said a word. I guess we'll never know.

I pause for a moment to examine Hazel's face as she says this. I remember hearing about a case like this happening in the 1920s or 30s, but I never knew who the kid was who helped the officer get in. Hazel smirks just a little before going back to Rolly. She knows who did it too.

The police officer didn't let Rolly go home by himself. He kept him with one of the ladies who lived in the building until he could interview him and then take him to mama. Rolly didn't mind—he just played with Murphy outside until all was clear. He was there for hours.

Mama and Mr. Bellamy had just come from the meeting where the papers for the merger or acquisition or whatever it was were officially signed. Successful meetings put Mr. Bellamy in a good mood—he was a great negotiator, and always got his way. They got

back from the conference center and went to get messages from Mrs.
Denning.

"Wait," Mrs. Denning stopped them from going into
Bellamy's office. Her face was tight and her shoulders were nearly up
by her ears. "There's someone here for you, Linda. I had him wait in
Mr. Bellamy's office. Sorry, sir."

"Who is it?" Bellamy asked before mama could say a word.
He started to move past her before Mrs. Denning answered.

The secretary cleared her throat and lowered her voice to
mama. "The police."

Mr. Bellamy stopped. Mama's eyes got real wide; the police
visiting was never a good thing. She shoved the paperwork that was
in her hands into Mr. Bellamy's instead, moving so quickly for his
office that he was left standing at Mrs. Denning's desk in shock. He
peeked through his doorway and saw mama talking to the officer,
catching a glimpse of Rolly's little legs kicking idly from the corner
of the room.

"What's this about?" Bellamy leaned closer to Mrs. Denning.

She kept that low and nervous tone, even wringing her hands
together like she could feel mama's anxiety from the other side of the
room. "Her boy helped the police find a dead body."

He didn't know which words were more alarming—*her boy*
or *dead body*. Apparently he assumed he'd get further with, "Her boy?"

"Yeah, little Rolland there. I don't know how he got so far

out—the officer said he was on the other side of town. Boy shoulda been in school..." she rambled before she looked back at Mr. Bellamy's face. His eyebrows were wrinkled as he looked at Rolly. "You never knew, sir?"

Mr. Bellamy shook his head. "I never knew she was married. He can't be Priestley's. Am I to assume he's her....lover?"

Mrs. Denning's jaw dropped. "No," she said emphatically. "Linda would never be unfaithful. Calvin's a beau—she has no husband, sir. Not anymore. A girl like her would never do a thing like that."

Bellamy set the papers on the desk and put both hands in his pockets. It was his stern examination stance. There was a little backwards lean in the way he stood too, like he was getting a better view of the situation at hand; letting it stew over in his mind. He was a deep thinker, Mr. Bellamy was.

"Her husband left her when little Rolland was very young," Mrs. Denning kept on defending. "Ending up dying on the railroad somewhere in the middle of nowhere. But that's why she hired me, sir. Both our husbands abandoned us....just in very different ways. She was looking out for me. She's a good kid, sir."

"I know that," Bellamy exhaled, smiling just a little bit at Rolly's funny faces—he was still reenacting his heroic act in his mind, rethinking ways he could've dramatically landed and flung the door open to rescue the local villagers from the security of the lock.

Mrs. Denning watched Mr. Bellamy for a moment, looking from him to Rolly and then back to him. "I could watch Rolland, if you want, while you two finish things up for the day," she offered.

Instead of answering her, Mr. Bellamy strolled into his office and stood squarely in front of Rolly. Mama saw this, quickly thanked the officer, and then turned to apologize.

"I'm so sorry, sir. This never hap—"

"I never knew you had children, Miss Sawyer."

Mama's eyes fell to her hands. She was massaging them, unable to find the words to express why she kept Rolly such a secret. "I'm sorry, I didn't think it was relevant to my work."

Bellamy offered Rolly a gentleman's handshake, paired with an "I'm Russell Bellamy," but he was cut off because Rolly had no concept of decorum back then.

"I know who you are," Rolly took the hand and shook it as hard as he could, asserting dominance and making the grown man chuckle. "You're the dragon."

"*Mr. Bellamy*," mama corrected, trying to shut him up.

"Right," Rolly nodded once and returned to his funny faces.

"The pleasure is mine," Bellamy responded. Mama couldn't tell if he was smiling or grimacing—it was something in between, I think—at Rolly's terrible manners. He took his hand away from him and put it back in his pocket, doing that contemplative lean again. "How old are you, Rolland?"

"I didn't know dragons were psychic."

"*Rolland*," mama hissed under her breath.

"We are, actually," Mr. Bellamy surprised her and didn't skip a beat. "That's what makes us great businessmen."

Rolly squinted at the dragon, trying to see the eyes through the scales. Bellamy's eyes were dark, but weren't as cold as Rolly expected from a dragon. He could see why mama thought so though. Men in three piece suits with pocket watches and ties always seemed cold on the outside. Like mannequins.

"I'm eight," Rolly eventually revealed, once he deemed the dragon temporarily harmless.

"I can get him home and come back if you need me to, sir," mama pressed. She didn't like having Rolly there; it made her anxious. She stopped massaging her hands and lifted Rolly up out of the chair by his arm. Instead of waiting for Mr. Bellamy to give her an answer, mama dragged Rolly back to Mrs. Denning's desk. "Where was Calvin?"

"I don't know, mama. I don't know," Rolly insisted, hoping he wasn't in any kind of trouble.

Mama sighed and bent down to look him in the eye. "I have work to do. I can't have you here, sweetheart, but I can't have you wandering in strange neighborhoods either." She straightened his collar, shaking her head. "Calvin should've taken you home if you weren't at school—why did he take you so far out?"

"Where did the officer find him?" Bellamy leaned against his door-frame. When mama told him the neighborhood, his face changed. As Rolly saw it, the dragon recognized that Rolly beat bad guys and decided he didn't want him and the toy gun on his belt in his castle anymore. He was done being nice.

"I wasn't by myself though, mama," Rolly tried to defend himself. "I had Murphy with me."

Mrs. Denning's eyes widened with curiosity. "And who's Murphy?" she asked before mama could.

"My dog."

"You don't have a dog," mama told him.

He shook his head. "I found him today and Cal let me keep him. We bought him a treat before I lost him. Before I lost Cal, not Murphy. Murphy stayed with me the whole time. He's a noble steed."

"Where is he now?"

"The doorman wouldn't let him inside your work, mama, so he said he'd watch Murphy outside."

Bellamy had heard enough, apparently. "Take your son home, Miss Sawyer," he said rather impatiently. "There's been enough excitement for one day."

Rolly jumped at the opportunity he now had to show Murphy to mama. Mama wasn't so thrilled to be dismissed, but she put on her coat, picked up her purse, and took Rolly's hand, letting him lead her to the noble steed.

When they got home, Calvin was in the kitchen waiting for them. Miss Hollis could never kick him out because it wasn't her place, so he would help himself to the kitchen, make himself something to eat, leave the mess for her to clean, and then help himself to more as he chose.

Mama didn't have the heart to kick Murphy to the curb, so she let Rolly take her in the house, as long as they went straight to his room and didn't come out until dinner. Rolly obeyed, because he could sense the trouble. Mama marched straight to the kitchen, and then all Rolly heard was shouting.

Some was mama. Some was Calvin. One of them threw a plate, and then mama gasped. The commotion made Murphy hide under Rolly's bed. Rolly crouched down to comfort her, but the noise scared him a little too. Heroes don't show fear, though. They're brave and strong; so Rolly reached for Murphy's furry gray head and whispered to her,

"Be brave, Murph. Be brave like me."

The noise died down just a bit, and Calvin's tone shifted. Rolly recognized his new voice—it was smooth and soft. Mama had started crying, and that was usually when the sweet promises came out. Probably because Rolly tended to make himself within earshot whenever mama's tears fell. Calvin's voice was low, but Rolly could catch a few sentences here and there.

"If we're gonna have a life together, I need to be able to

61

support you. You know that, right?" he heard him say. Mama
whimpered what sounded like a *yes*, so Calvin went on. "I'm going to
take care of you—you just have to stop asking so many questions.
Rolly was fine. He was with the dog, and she looks like she can hold
her own."

Rolly guffawed and glanced over at Murphy, who had
listened to him and become brave enough to crawl out from under
the bed. "You're a girl?" he asked her incredulously. "I can't even
believe this, Murph."

He then heard some light scuffling, like mama was sitting on
the floor and Calvin was helping her stand back up. Rolly cracked
open his bedroom door to take a peek. He saw Calvin kiss mama on
the mouth. Mama didn't deep smile, but she tried to.

She told him, "I'll see what I can do."

And Cal kissed her again and left for the night.

It wasn't mama who came to Rolly's room for bedtime. It
was Miss Hollis. Her sleeves were rolled up, her apron was wet from
the dishes, and her mouth was twisted—and not in that teasing smile
she normally wore.

"Mama's resting," Rolly concluded.

"That's right, baby," Hollis nodded. "Now let's get you ready
to rest yourself too."

Rolly sighed and ruffled the top of Murphy's head while he
made his way around his room, gathering his pajamas and putting his

toy gun in its rightful home on the shelf. "It's because we got so lost today, Murph. Mama's not happy."

Miss Hollis grunted, following him and picking up his dirty clothes as he made it through his routine around the room. "It's got nothin' to do with you, child."

"Was it the bleeding man I helped?"

"Nope." Miss Hollis's jaw clenched. "It was the man who lost you, boy. Now get into bed and tell me the next part of mama's story."

Rolly did as he was told, climbing into bed, with Murphy finding her favorite place quickly beside him. "I can tell mama this part tomorrow. The princess met a noble steed—one loyal and brave and ready to help save her from the dragon. But the steed wasn't allowed in the castle, because it could poop on the floor. So the prince got the steed a yummy apple from the marketplace, and from then on, the steed was true."

"Sounds like a good pet to me," Hollis gave him a smile.

"Not a pet," Rolly shook his head. "A best friend. Every hero needs a best friend."

Aunt Hazel reaches for another cookie.

"I don't know how old she was at the time, but Murphy seemed to

live forever. I have a picture from Rolly's wedding reception, and I'm pretty sure she's in the background." She takes the photo album from me again, frantically thumbing through each page, scanning for her brother's wedding.

"Is your dad in any of these pictures?" I ask.

Abruptly, she shuts the album. "You're jumping ahead, young lady," she shakes her head sternly. She decides to keep the album close, probably so I don't peak and find the answer for myself. Mindlessly, she strokes the cover and stares off into the distance.

"I have a feeling we're getting to that part soon," Juliet says softly— mostly to me, but Hazel hears and narrows her eyes just a little.

"Not as soon as you'd hope," she corrects. "But we're closer than we were. The princess needs to be saved first."

Of course.

I nod, check the battery on my recorder, and hold it back up as she hugs the photo album against her chest. Let's save the princess.

the quest

Mama hated doing this. But she promised Calvin she would. Honestly, Mr. Bellamy wasn't quite sure how to respond. He probably sat staring at her for a few painstaking minutes before he answered. Meanwhile, she sat massaging her hands in her lap, bracing herself.

Bellamy had that same contemplative lean when he was sitting behind his desk as he did when he was standing. Except, instead of sliding his hands in his pockets, he held one hand near his face, tapping his mouth lightly.

"What sort of work has he done in the past?"

Mama hesitated. "Most recently, he's been a courier. Before that, I think he worked a little in construction."

Bellamy nodded very slowly, soaking in the clear signs of mama's anxiety. Her legs were crossed, and the bottom one bounced like a Pogo stick on caffeine. He closed his eyes for a moment, in a way that made mama think he was gonna shoot her down with his fire breath.

"How long have you known him?"

Mama shrugged. She was never sure. Calvin told her they'd known each other for years, because he met her at the train station where Rolly's papa left her. Mama remembered it differently, but she said what she'd been told.

"For years, now," she said. "We met shortly after my late husband...."

"Left you."

66

"He died," she tried to correct.

"After he left you," Mr. Bellamy pointed his hand in her direction. "He abandoned you and your newborn child. Is that when Mr. Priestley entered the picture? When you were already broken."

The eyes went back to the hands. Mama knew what he meant. I'm sure she worried his keen judge of character would keep him from giving a man like Cal a position of any kind in his company. "Yeah, that's when I met Calvin."

Bellamy shook his head and drew his hand back in near his face. "Why is it that you keep letting this happen, Miss Sawyer? These men, they chain you up and drop you. And you let them. When will you learn?" he added in a deep mumble, probably more to himself than mama.

He wasn't always the nicest back then. Believe it or not, he was always the nicest to mama. Years later, mama said it was probably good for her. No one told hard truths like Mr. Bellamy. It helped her learn; she picked herself up, dusted herself off, and got back to work.

"I guess....I never will," she shrugged again. "He's not always an upstanding gentleman, but he's decent. Resourceful. Thinks well on his feet. He's also very innovative. I think, given the chance, he could be a valuable asset to you and this company."

I was never sure if it was the way mama's back straightened when she dusted herself off and went back to work, or the alarming way her tone changed when she forced herself to lie. It doesn't matter though. What matters is that Mr. Bellamy noticed both, and they pushed him back into that contemplative lean.

He rubbed his face, inhaled sharply and paused. "I suppose there could be a position for him here...somewhere," he finally said. "Mrs. Denning could always use help with the filing, so you don't have to use up every free moment you have."

Mama sighed in embarrassment. "You've seen that, huh?"

"Yes, I have. And as sweet as it is, it's hardly productive. You're more valuable than a mindless paper pusher," he shifted forward in his seat, lowering his intimidating stare. "But Mr. Priestley could be suitable."

"So you'll make him an offer?"

His own dark eyes tightened when he saw the relief in mama's baby blues. "I'll consider it," he told her. He stood to go for the door, but stopped when he was right beside mama. "But, before I do," he added softly, "Do you actually love him, Miss Sawyer?"

The question must've surprised mama because she took a long pause before responding. Her face flushed a bit and her eyes went down to her hands again. But then she made up her mind and looked back up at him, her lying voice restored. "Of course I do," she settled.

"Hm," was all Mr. Bellamy said before opening the door and calling for Calvin to come. Cal was sitting on the bench near Mrs.

Denning's desk, complimenting her and making charming small talk while he waited on mama to *"work her magic."*

When Mr. Bellamy offered him the job of assistant secretary, and even held a hand out to congratulate him, Calvin beamed. "I'll be the best thing for this company, sir. I can guarantee it."

"Hm," Bellamy said again. "Mrs. Denning will train you," he gestured in the secretary's direction. "I'm sure you'll be...*decent.*"

Calvin got off of work at an hour more decent than he was. Well, everybody did but mama. And Mr. Bellamy. And sometimes Mrs. Denning. But Calvin was a nobody in the company, so he left at 5 every day. He promised mama he'd meet her at the house and make sure Rolly made it home from school. She was giving him another chance—mama was full of second chances. Rolly was instructed to meet Cal outside the Bellamy Building, waiting patiently with Murphy. When he got there, he saw Cal standing close to the street, with that same bald man he saw at the park.

Calvin seemed excited, so Rolly moved closer to them, wanting to see what all the fuss was about. However, the bald man was not amused. He had his arms crossed in front of his chest and his eyebrows raised higher than the skyscraper towering over them. Rolly hesitated to tell Cal he was ready to go and instead stood quietly for a moment or two until the men were finished talking. Cal had the same puffy-chested look that Rolly had when he finished shooting fake dragons in the eye. Unlike mama's usual congratulatory, tired smile, the bald man was grimacing.

"I'll see what he says, I guess," he told Calvin. "Stumped cops is good, but O'Shea's not so easy to impress."

Cal moved his hands like he was going to say something more, but then caught sight of Rolly standing behind them.

"Oh, hey kid," he motioned him over. "You ready?" Rolly smiled and pranced the distance between them, Murphy trotting behind.

Bald Man did a little wave and then said, "That the secretary's kid you were talkin' about?" out of the corner of his mouth.

"Executive assistant," Cal corrected, pulling Rolly in by the shoulders, as if displaying him proudly. "And he's good, Alby. Trust me."

"Who are you?" Rolly asked too loudly.

The bald man smirked. "He just told ya, kid. Name's Alby."

Like the gentleman his mama raised, Rolly held out a hand for Alby to shake. "Rolland Sawyer, sir," he said politely.

"Alright, let's go," Cal moved him past the bald man. Rolly didn't understand why he couldn't sit and chat with the man, but he didn't dare question Cal's earnest.

On the brisk walk home Rolly drilled Calvin with questions, as kids do. And Rolly's a persistent one. Kid never *didn't* have questions. Every time mama told him anything, he'd have at least two follow-up questions in the barrel, ready to be shot. Cal's impatience was running high, though.

"Look, kid," he finally shut him up, "it's all part of my plan. Okay? Just trust me."

"You have a plan?" You see, Rolly was never judgmental, he just liked knowing stuff. He never doubted that Cal had a plan—he just wanted to be in on it.

"Of course I do," Cal strutted. "A plan every man should have, Rolly. I'm gonna find my fortune....very soon."

"And then you'll get rich and marry mama?"

Cal's strut slowed a little. When he didn't answer right away, Rolly stopped and waited. Cal turned on his heel and shrugged casually, brushing off his hesitation. "Sure, maybe one day."

Rolly nodded in agreement. "You'd have to save her from the dragon first, though," he pointed at him.

Calvin chuckled.

"What's so funny?"

"How do you think I'm gonna find my fortune, kid?" Cal strode ahead of him, leaving Rolly stunned only a few steps behind.

"You're gonna storm the castle for the secret gold!" he ran and leapt in front of him.

"Shh!" Cal covered Rolly's mouth almost before his feet hit the sidewalk.

"Oh don't worry," he brushed Cal's hand away. "I won't tell anyone. We don't want the dragon gettin' wise of the plan and adding trebuchets or something."

Cal frowned. "Trebuchets?"

Rolly loved informing people of the intricacies of medieval warfare. For some reason. Even at eight years old, the boy was a regular self-taught scholar. He even adjusted the collar of his shirt before diving into his explanation. "They're kinda like guns, except no bullets. They launch things from the top of castles to hit the soldiers on the other side of the walls. Things like rocks, dead bodies, debris, really any—"

"Yeah, don't tell anybody, okay?"

"Does mama know?"

Cal put a finger to his lips. "Don't worry about mama. Mamas always know everything. Just don't talk about it to anyone else."

Rolly so swore. "Mama really does know everything, doesn't she?" he added. "She's the smartest lady."

"Sure she is, kid. Sure she is."

"So Calvin robbed Bellamy?" I ask. My excitement is growing and I

can't really wait for the end of the story. Some of these names are only vaguely ringing a bell. I now regret not listening to all of Grandpa Rolly's stories.

He was talking all the time, since I was a kid up until he died a few years ago. I loved his jokes, but in all honesty, I ended up tuning out most of his stories. My older sisters were a little better about listening to the old man, and now I wish I had been too.

The ones I remember didn't have all of these names, though. At least, I don't think. Could be wrong. Maybe this story was just for Aunt Hazel. She seems to thrive on it, and none of it really sounds familiar enough for me to assume he told it to the kids before.

I love how personal it all is to her.

I love imagining Grandpa Rolly as a child, just as energetic as he was when he was ninety years old. Just as chatty. Just as adventurous. Just as adoring.

I don't want anything else to go wrong in this story, but something in Aunt Hazel's tone tells me it's not going to get any better yet.

Especially when she mentions the troll.

"He tried to rob Bellamy," Aunt Hazel clarifies. "But not yet. Does Russell Bellamy seem the kinda man who lets himself get robbed? It's not in his blood. Besides, his cousin wouldn't allow it."

the quest

the troll

There were a lotta bosses in that town. A lotta bosses, with a lotta underground dealings. O'Shea was just one fish in a busy pond. But he was a well-connected fish. He had hands in the pockets of politicians, law enforcement, and successful businessmen.

The one businessman he wanted in his corner, though, wouldn't budge. Not even playing the family card could convince him. Russell Bellamy may have come off as a rude snob but, boy, was that man steadfast and upstanding in his own ways.

Bellamy would sit at his desk with that contemplative leaning posture, rubbing his mouth with his hand, absorbing the offer O'Shea brought to him every time he dropped by. Nothing would make a difference.

"I'm not a loan shark, Jimmy. I'm a businessman," he'd tell him, over and over and over again.

O'Shea did what a lot of mobsters did back then: he'd give loans to poor souls who found themselves broke and unemployed— and that was most common-folk in those days too—then hike up the interest rates.

"Come on," O'Shea chided him. "We're family. What's blood good for?"

O'Shea took his mama's last name when he made his own way in the mafia, you see. Told people he was a feared name in his own right, not because of the career his father made for himself. He thrived during Prohibition, but when that was all over, there was room in the new market for what the officials called "predatory lending." He'd use his bootlegging money and loan them to families and businesses looking for help. When they couldn't pay the high interest rates, he'd take a big cut from the business profits, or break the legs of the man of the house.

It was cruel but effective, ya know. It kept him making money. Who do you think got paid first when money finally hit? The man breaking legs and exploiting businesses.

Bellamy was unmoved. He didn't care how promising the endeavor sounded. "And if the economy doesn't improve?" he posed.

O'Shea leaned back in his chair on the opposite side of the desk. It was a genetic lean, I think. "It always does."

"Let's say it doesn't. Let's say these people stop earning money and stop paying the interest. There are only so many legs that can be broken. I don't see how targeting those who can barely afford to live is a strong enough guarantee to be worth my investment."

"Their inability to stay afloat is exactly why it's the perfect time," O'Shea leaned forward again, pressing his hands together for emphasis. "We're the heroes right now. The heroes they're gonna owe everything once things get better. How are we any different than banks? They're just lousy crooks who pretend to follow laws."

Bellamy rolled his eyes. "You're wasting my time again, Jimmy."

O'Shea laughed heartily, knowing exactly how little progress he'd made this time. Honorably defeated, he stood and straightened his suit coat. "You need to take more risks, Russ."

"I take plenty of risks. They're just studied and well-informed. That's why I make more money than you," Bellamy jabbed. He was playful sometimes. Not often, but sometimes.

"Keep it in the family, they tell me."

"Jimmy," Bellamy held up a hand. "For what it's worth, if I saw you begging in the streets, I would buy you a steak dinner."

With a dulcet grin on his face, but his eyes still squinted in annoyance, O'Shea saluted his cousin. "I'll take it," he said. On his way out he ran into mama who was heading in with the final plans for a gala celebrating the acquisition for Bellamy to approve. "Ah, the lovely Miss Sawyer," he stopped to kiss her hand as she passed.

"Oh, hello," mama blushed.

"We met not a week ago," he reminded her.

"I remember, Mr. O'Shea," she smiled politely.

Bellamy cleared his throat loudly from inside the office. "Good day, O'Shea."

Noting that he had been thoroughly dismissed, O'Shea bowed his head to mama, gave her a wink, and left the office. Mama waved as he moved past her; she caught sight of the way Calvin nodded and then slowly followed the mobster into the hallway. Pretending she didn't notice, mama turned to Mrs. Denning, who was grinning from ear to ear.

"Did ya see that, doll?" she whispered giddily to mama. "He thought you were stunning."

"Oh no," mama swatted her playfully with the folder. "He's just friendly. I'm not the type to catch someone's eye like that, Margie, you know that."

Mrs. Denning shrugged inconspicuously. "In the right dress you could be. Men like seeing *more* of you."

"That's the spirit," Mr. Bellamy chimed in, suddenly appearing in the doorway. He was waiting impatiently for the folder mama was supposed to have brought him. "The mother of a young boy should always show as much of her body to the public as possible."

"I'm sorry, sir," Mrs. Denning stammered. "I didn't mean—"

"Well then what do you suggest?" mama put her hand on her hips, keeping the folder angled away from him.

He sighed, now part of the conversation he was trying to cut short. "That completely depends on the type of someone whose eye you hope to catch."

"A charming and wealthy man of class."

Bellamy glanced mama up and down for a moment before saying, "Then I suggest you get back to work." Swiftly, he swiped the folder out of her hand and went back to his office.

Mrs. Denning frowned. "He wasn't very helpful at all," she muttered.

Mama chuckled, patting Mrs. Denning's arm, and followed Mr. Bellamy into the office.

"Is everything ready?" he said, keeping his eyes on the paperwork in his hand.

"Yes," mama said taking her usual seat near his desk, crossing one leg over the other, ready for business. "The caterers have been arranged, guests have received their invitations, and the orchestra has been...contacted."

"Contacted? Not confirmed?"

Mama made a face.

"What is it?" he demanded.

"I was thinking we could explore an option a little more....contemporary. Like a jazz band, maybe a vocalist—"

"No," he cut her off. He closed the folder and looked her intently in the eye. "We've always had an orchestra. Our guests expect it."

Mama cocked her head to one side, unmoved by his opinion. "Yes well, it could be time for a change. Jazz is all the rage and it's much easier to dance to."

And he leaned back again. This time, his expression was significantly more critical than before. "You know, the waltz was invented before jazz was even thought of. And it suited society just fine."

"I'm not disagreeing, sir. The waltz is great. I'm only saying that something with a little more life to it might be more encouraging to new partners and hires than a droning violin." Mama sighed, not caring what he had to say next. "But, if it's what you prefer, I will arrange the orchestra to play."

It was moments like these that made Mr. Bellamy wonder why mama ever let men like Calvin push her around. Mama always said it was because when she was at work she wasn't a woman pining for a husband, she was a loyal assistant. She wasn't a woman and he wasn't a man. It made it easier for her, I suppose, to voice opinions and get things done. Didn't help the spilling over her emotions, which sometimes happened after a hard day, but it sure helped her tell Bellamy exactly what she was thinking—the best businessmen value that kind of honesty from intelligent people, no matter who they are.

Rolly described these parts as the princess being brave—she was never scared of the dragon. She respected how dangerous he was, but she never let him see her afraid. You can't let the dragon get too cocky about his wild amount of power, Rolly would say.

Since he got what he wanted, Mr. Bellamy didn't argue any further, and just watched her rise to call the orchestra manager. "Miss Sawyer," he called.

She turned curtly, frustrated and ready for his next order. The bottom of her brown dress whipped around her legs almost as sharply as her blonde curls hit her cheeks. He stared for a moment;

she always wore such dull, subdued colors. They were high quality dresses, sure, but she never picked the ones that grab the attention.

"I had your dress tailored. See that it's picked up before the gala"

"The blue one?"

"The purple."

"You mean burgundy."

"No, I mean purple."

Mama cocked her head again.

He lifted the front of the folder again, giving the plans another glance. "It's a new business venture, Miss Sawyer. It requires a fresh look and a fresh start. There will be many to impress."

"Will Mr. O'Shea be attending?" Bellamy's eyes snapped up at her, flaring until he saw her lightly chuckle. "Of course I'll have the clothes picked up. I sent your suit to be pressed, too. The gray one."

"You know best," he replied.

"Don't say that too loudly," mama smiled feebly. "People won't believe a word you say."

Mama had a lot of formal gowns for someone living like she did—and Mr. Bellamy bought every one of them. I used to steal them from her closet and try them on in front of the mirror. Even when the times changed, they never went out of style. Mr. Bellamy had the best taste and he always knew what would look best on mama. She had pink ones and black ones and gold ones and green ones. They were all floor length—he only picked the dresses she wore to fancy business events. Very elegant. I suppose he figured if he's paying for all of them, he might as well like the look of them.

Spending the afternoon at the tailor's was typical right before a big to-do. Mama usually left work early and did it on her own, but Mr. Bellamy suggested she take Rolly with her. He called him "Rolland," though. No one else really called him by his full first name. Mr. Bellamy was a very proper fellow and he thought a young man should be called by his given name.

So mama took Rolly to the tailor with her; she was fitted in her beautiful new purple dress, while he advanced Murphy's training just outside the shop. He had her jump and roll over, and all of those normal dog things, with a few noble steed tricks too—like the proper stance when facing an enemy and how to bite a dragon on command. Silly things like that.

Meanwhile, passing the shop on the other side of the street, Murphy recognized Calvin walking along with a lady and barked twice. Rolly waved his arms and hollered. Looking as though he had suddenly found what he was looking for, Calvin pointed and waved at Rolly then guided the lady with him across the busy street.

"Hey, kid," he said. He patted Murphy on the head, but she dodged his touch and stepped behind Rolly. Cal smoothed past it and moved that hand behind the lady's back again instead. "This is my sister, Anita."

Anita was a scheming modern broad. A pants-wearing, lip-smacking, hair-cropped short kinda gal. She was very different from mama, and she never let her forget that. Anita was a jazz singing activist—not a famous one, and not regularly employed. She made enough to treat Calvin to lunch every now and then, but her paychecks were spotty. That didn't stop her, though. She still sang her heart out, thinking she was the most alluring songbird there ever was, as if the louder she sang, the more the world would agree with her.

Mama told me her causes weren't necessarily the bad part, it was her delivery. She was always mocking mama's desperation for a husband, criticizing her aversion to pantsuits, and told her she'd probably catch a man if she didn't try so hard. Called her "old-fashioned" and "dull."

As you can imagine, she wasn't my mama's favorite person.

But again, that didn't stop her.

Anita crouched down to Rolly's eye-line and smiled real big at him. "Well aren't you adorable," she mused.

Rolly squinted and frowned. "You don't look anything like him."

Anita was even more confused than Rolly was. "Don't look like who?"

"Cal," he said. "I thought you were his sister."

"Not all siblings look alike," she explained, standing back up and looking at him down the slope of her nose. It's true. Rolly and I look nothing like each other. Never did—I always favored papa's side of the family, while Rolly's relation to mama was undeniable.

"I've never had a sister before, so I guess you're probably right." Rolly then turned his back to them and continued the training of the noble Murphy.

Calvin cleared his throat and muttered, "She's probably inside," to his sister.

Anita ran a hand over her smooth, short curls and scoffed. "Do you really think she'd do it? She's just the secretary."

"Executive assistant," Calvin whispered. "I just need time to warm her up to it."

Just then, mama stepped out, finished with her fitting, and with the promise of a finished product. At seeing Anita standing there near Rolly, with Calvin at her side, mama held her purse just a little tighter to her coat.

"Anita," she acknowledged.

Anita just smirked. "Doing a little shopping?"

"Can I help you with something?"

Calvin stepped in front of his sister, attempting to soften mama's tight mouth. "We were having lunch and I wanted to see the dress you'd be wearing to the gala."

"Oh," mama was a little surprised. "Are you going?"

Cal chuckled. "Well, the whole office is invited to represent the company. So yes, I intend to go. Unless you'd rather go with someone else?"

Mama shook her head quickly. "No, no. I'd love for you to go."

Kissing her on the cheek, like a tease, Cal winked at her. "We can dance the night away."

"Only if you like to waltz," mama sighed. Anita snorted, but mama ignored her. "Mr. Bellamy insisted on an orchestra."

Calvin took a step back and glanced at his sister. "Well, Linda, aren't you the one making the arrangements? You should hire Anita. Sneak a little jazz in there."

"Add a little good taste to the poor man's palette," Anita chimed in. "Rescue his guests from being bored to tears."

"I'm afraid he's already made his decision."

"C'mon," Anita leaned in a little closer to mama. "A pretty thing like you could convince him of anything, right? Just put on that dress he bought you and give him a good talking to."

"Have you ever met Mr. Bellamy?" mama asked her, crossing her arms in front of her chest. "He can't be convinced of anything. Better than me have tried."

"None of them know him like you do. He's the only man you haven't thrown yourself at so he hasn't been scared off just yet. That's gotta count for something, now, hasn't it?"

Mama's mouth tightened again.

Again, Cal cut in before mama could respond. He was always
so much better at talking to her than Anita was; I don't really
understand why he brought her along in the first place—she only
made things worse.

"He'd-he'd tell you things, if you'd ask," he took her aside and
stood between the ladies.

"What does that have to do with the orchestra?" mama
snapped.

He placed both hands on her shoulders and held her in front
of him, looking her square in the eye. "Remember when I said I'll be
falling into a fortune that'll take us away from here? I met with Mr.
O'Sh—"

"I don't wanna know, Cal," mama held her hand up and
waved him away. He only grabbed her shoulders and held her still
again. "I don't want to know," she enunciated. "You've involved me
enough already."

He stared hard at her for a good long minute before
believing her. He let her go and sighed deeply. "Okay, then. If you
won't do it, and you won't get Anita hired...then I'm bringing her as
my guest to the gala."

"What?"

"Someone's gotta schmooze, honey," Anita crooned. "If it's
not gonna be you, then I'm more than happy to step up."

"Fine," mama grabbed Rolly's hand and brushed past Cal.

"Fine. Take your sister. Do whatever it is you're planning to do. I won't stop you."

Mama didn't think Rolly was paying much attention during that whole incident. He was off playing with Murphy the whole time. But little boys hear more than they seem too. Always.

After mama cleaned him up, fed him dinner, and tucked him into bed, she continued their bedtime story. It had been a few nights since mama got to tell it herself. Rolly was so used to making up the new parts and catching her up later that he told her he had already figured out what happened next.

"Oh, have you?"

Rolly patted the side of his bed, because you can't continue the story without the noble steed paying complete attention. Murphy hopped onto the bed, in between mama and Rolly, so Rolly could clear his throat and begin,

"Well, the prince has to save the princess, right? Not only did he learn about the dragon's castle, but he found out about the dragon's hidden gold, too. So he decided that he would sneak into the castle, trick the dragon, take his gold, and use the gold to save the princess."

"Wait, wait," mama slowed him down. Rolly talked fast when he was excited. And telling stories always got him excited. "You think the prince is going to steal the dragon's gold?"

"Yes, but first he has to find out where it's hidden in the castle." Mama closed her eyes, which alarmed Rolly. "What's wrong? Is that not how the story goes?"

Mama sighed. "No, you're probably right. I was just afraid that's what was happening."

"Why does that scare you, mama? The prince is going to save the princess with that gold."

Mama pressed her lips together. She was skeptical, and Rolly didn't like mama not believing his story. "How can gold save the princess, sweetheart?"

It took him a moment, but after wrinkling his face in thought, he decided on an answer. "The prince could use the gold to buy the princess her own castle so when they sneak out of the dragon's keep, she has a place to hide and live in safety."

Mama couldn't argue with that. She wanted to, but she couldn't. The dragon's gold would solve a lot of the problems she thought she had—the prince would have found his fortune and would probably marry the princess. And Rolly was right, they could afford a castle of their own.

It's what the princess wanted.

She thought, at least.

Hazel doesn't inspire much faith in her mother's judgment. My mom told me before I left for this visit to be careful what I asked about. Apparently Aunt Hazel was once married, but only for two years before he was killed in Vietnam. She hit a lot of lows after being widowed—I remember Grandpa Rolly mentioning a few times his "poor sister Hazel." But grandpa helped her come out of it, and she actually went on to live a good life.

I probably know enough to write her story myself, but mom thought hearing it all from her would be a lot more meaningful and correctly sourced.

If there's anything Aunt Hazel was, it was a romantic like Grandpa Rolly. She may disguise it with her skepticism, but they were cut from the same cloth nonetheless. Clearly she didn't see her mother as a romantic. Every time she mentions her mama's desperation for marriage, she has an edge in her voice, like Linda was a traitor to her gender. Not because of her wanting to be married, but because she no longer cared about love— she wanted convenience.

She hasn't said so just yet, but I suspect Aunt Hazel will start to change her tone soon.

Hazel never remarried in her entire sixty one years of widowhood. She has photos of Uncle Drew strewn throughout her house, even though he's too painful to talk about. Grandpa Rolly called them a "love for the ages."

I hope mama finds that. I have a feeling she will. What's the point of starting this story if Hazel wasn't building up for an epic tale of love?

I have my own theories, but I don't dare interrupt her. She's getting to the good part.

the troll

the ball

the ball

During the Depression, the poor hit the streets and the rich hit the ballrooms. What better way to fuel your company with hope than to throw a lavish party? Bellamy's acquisition with whatever company he had just bought out was something to celebrate, you know. He created more job opportunities at an entry level, and gave promotions to the loyal employees in the middle who now had to take on more work. He did great things—I'm telling you, he was a stellar businessman.

And everyone wanted to attend a Bellamy Company party. Upper and middle management, as well as his personal office staff, were invited. Board members from the now-deceased company, as well as investors in his own thriving company were also invited. Politicians and appropriate stockholders were among the guests there too. It was a big to-do.

Mama was done up in her stunning purple dress—mama wasn't used to looking stunning. She was beautiful, but in a more adorable sort of way. But in that dress and her golden hair smoothed up in a French roll, she wowed the crowd. Calvin and Anita being there didn't help her nerves, though. Her shoulders were nearly to her ears from the moment they entered the main hall of the Bellamy building.

Anita wore a bright green dress that was loud enough to catch every eye there, and a laugh that was even louder. Calvin did his job and introduced her to all the high rollers—even the ones he had never met before—so she could turn on the charm. The only one she had a hard time getting to was Mr. Bellamy himself. He was always surrounded by the highest of rollers who amused and joked with each other for the first couple of hours without reprieve.

I don't know what they would talk about for hours, but Rolly guessed it was all to do with money. I think he's mistaken. Papa said the interests of poor men and rich men really aren't that different. They still like baseball, politics, women, and the weather. Among other things, I'd imagine. Whatever Mr. Bellamy was talking about, it was mighty interesting. Believe it or not, he could captivate an audience when he wanted to. It was unexpected charisma from a man so typically severe.

Anita thought the best way to get his attention was to talk loudly within earshot. She was pretty enough, a man would hear her, see her, then give her his undivided attention. Girls do this all the time—you know that. It doesn't always work. To her credit, though, Bellamy did hear her.

"I sang a gig like this last month in New Jersey at the governor's re-election celebration. His assistant knew how to book a party, let me tell you," she crooned.

One of the foolish old men chuckled heartily. "It's a wonder Bellamy didn't book you for tonight."

Anita placed a modest hand to her chest. "Oh I don't fault Mr. Bellamy at all. He has impeccable taste. I only regret his assistant rejected the prospect before Mr. Bellamy got to hear a taste of what could have been."

"Miss Sawyer turned you away?" one of the younger businessmen said in surprise. "Tsk, shame on her."

"Who is that?" the older one squinted, not recalling if they meant mama or Mrs. Denning.

The man, who was probably aged between the two others, almost spoke up to answer but Anita beat him to it. Which he didn't like at all.

"That adorable little mousy thing over there," Anita pointed in mama's direction.

Mama never stopped working—she was bustling to and fro, making sure the caterers had everything taken care of, and then checking with the orchestra's manager to confirm closing time and such. Anything to keep her as far from Anita and Calvin as possible. Had she stopped to breathe for a few moments, the sight of her would have given Evil Queen Anita a run for her money.

"She's awfully competent. I'm sure there was a reason for the slight," the middle man assured Anita.

His name was Robert-or-Colin-or-something-Bonaventure, I think. He was one of the big bosses of the company Bellamy just bought—a hotel business, actually. He hoped to keep his job under Mr. Bellamy; he knew he was close enough to hear and he happened to like mama. Most people did. She was always sweet and accommodating to Mr. Bellamy's associates in the business world. "Bellamy always uses this orchestra."

"Oh of course, of course," she said. "Perhaps the next time she won't be quite so scatterbrained with the preparation and venture out a little."

"Well," the older man held up his glass of champagne, "to what could have been."

They all tapped their glasses together and Anita beamed, glancing obviously over to Mr. Bellamy, who continued to pretend she wasn't there. His eyes were actually watching mama. When Anita noticed this, she cleared her throat real loud and decided it was time for her next strategy—slinking past him so he could better see her figure in that dress. Girls do this all the time too, and they always have. Anita wasn't very original.

He sure didn't give her the up-and-down examination she was hoping for, but he did take notice of the men who followed her. He paused to shake Mr. Bonaventure's hand, nod at the old man, and completely ignore the younger man. Rich people don't have to be polite to people who insult their assistants.

Anita walked straight to her brother to complain about her failure. "He won't even look at me," she whispered to him. "And Linda's no help."

"She doesn't wanna be involved," he agreed.

"She would if you worked on her a little more."

"I do occasionally have to pretend to respect her wishes," he curled his lips.

"The self-righteous—"

"Anita."

Anita rolled her eyes. "You'll just have to snoop around for the vault."

"You really think he'd keep it here? I scoured this building the moment I got here—there's nothing." Calvin took a sip of his champagne when he noticed Bellamy glancing in their direction. He may not have been close enough to hear what they were saying, but Mr. Bellamy was no idiot. He could wager a guess. Calvin lifted his glass in salute and then lowered his head. "You have to get yourself invited to his house. That's probably where it is."

Anita pursed her lips and reached for the nearest glass on the nearest waiter's tray. "If I can manage that, I might as well marry the man. Then I could just hand the bars to you myself." She let out another charmingly fake laugh, hoping to keep Bellamy's eyes on her. "This better be worth it. If there's only two brick's worth, I'll—"

"You'll what?" Calvin challenged.

She considered for a moment. "I'll sell your little girlfriend for a few more, and you won't see an ounce of it."

The orchestra changed songs, a much louder one than before —catching Anita and Calvin off guard, and even diverting Mr. Bellamy's distant attention. The older gentleman from earlier approached Anita and asked her to dance. To avoid looking out of place and finally noticing mama was nowhere to be found, Calvin sought out another lady to dance with as well.

Mr. Bellamy glanced around the conductor, looking for where mama was bustling to now. But he couldn't see her either. The party was on the second floor, which had the most spacious hall for the dancing and frivolity and all that. Mr. Bellamy's office itself was on the fifth floor, far enough from all the noise that it was peaceful and quiet. The perfect place to hide when one has a headache—it had a small couch and everything.

It took Mr. Bellamy about five to ten minutes to find mama. She was sitting on the couch in his office, with her forehead resting in her palm and her elbow propped up on the arm of the couch. When she heard Mr. Bellamy come in she quickly sat up from her slump.

"Everything alright, Miss Sawyer?" he asked.

"Yes, yes," she moved to rise from the couch, but her body decided she'd better sit back down. "I was just resting for a few minutes. Is something wrong? Should I—?"

"No, not at all," he slipped his hands into his suit pockets. "You've earned a rest. I only wanted to thank you."

"For what?"

"Arranging the orchestra as I asked. And for not hiring Miss Priestley."

Hearing her name made mama rub her head. "Did she try to sell you on her act?"

Mr. Bellamy chuckled. "She presented her act, all right. She didn't have many great things to say about you."

"She never does."

He leaned against the side of his desk, facing mama. "A clever gold-digger would appeal to her target and compliment the things he cares about, rather than deprecating them. I have aspirin in my desk."

"I know. I already took a few, thank you. I'll be alright, sir. I usually am." Mama stopped rubbing her head, realizing how much attention she was drawing to it. "Anita's never seen much worth complimenting, I guess. Although, she did once call me sensible. Of course, she coupled that with *vulnerable* and *weak*."

"Plenty of men love vulnerability in women."

Mama sighed and smiled a little in spite of herself. "Well, that's a relief."

Mr. Bellamy cleared his throat, realizing he'd insulted her. So he leaned forward and asked, "Would you let your son get pushed around in the streets, Miss Sawyer?"

"What? No, of course not."

"Would you let him starve?"

"No, never."

"You'd do anything to see that he's taken care of?"

"Yes, I would."

"Even if it sacrifices your own comfort and happiness?"

Mama looked down at her hands. "Of course."

"Miss Priestley is wrong. You're not weak at all."

Mama looked back up at him; there wasn't a hint of teasing in his face. It was probably the softest she'd ever seen his eyes. She wasn't sure how to respond—she wasn't very comfortable with praise like that, not after hearing everything to the contrary for so long.

"It takes a very special person to put up with me for three years, Miss Sawyer," he said in a gentle tone. He then stood straighter and leaned back in that way he did. "A weak one would have quit by now. Miss Priestley wouldn't last a day."

Mama smirked, imagining Anita fumbling over papers and struggling to keep up with dictations. She stood and stepped over to his record player stand, distancing herself from the compliment. "One look at your taste in music and she'd quit within the hour."

Mr. Bellamy laughed and watched her. "That's probably true."

She thumbed through the records on the bottom shelf, illustrating her point. "Her own style isn't anything worth writing home about, but she'd argue that jazz is quite possibly...."

"The sloppiest genre," he finished for her, before noticing she'd frozen.

Mama slowly turned around, pulling a record from its place amongst the others. It was the French record mama suggested weeks ago. "What's this?"

Mr. Bellamy cleared his throat and moved forward to defend himself. "Lucienne Boyer."

"I know that." He tried to take it from her, but failed. Mama was too quick. She opened the sleeve and took out the vinyl. "How long have you had it?"

He sighed. "It was a...recent purchase." Mama raised her eyebrows at him. "It isn't jazz."

She giggled. "No, it isn't. But there's no orchestra either." She placed the vinyl on the phonograph and started playing the first track. As it began, she closed her eyes and smiled, while Mr. Bellamy kept on defending himself as he stepped toward the music.

"French melodies tend to forgive the lack of a full orchestra."

"This one's my favorite," she said softly. "*Parlez-moi d'amour.*"

"It makes a great waltz," he pointed out, still standing his stubborn ground.

Mama opened her eyes and glanced at him skeptically. "No, it doesn't."

Mr. Bellamy was rarely wrong, which means he had a reputation of being right to uphold, so he took his hands out of his pockets and offered one to mama. "Yes, it does. Here, I'll show you."

Before taking his hand, mama maintained that skeptical glare. "This is the only dance you know, isn't it? That's why you don't like jazz."

He waved his hand at her until she took it. He pulled her in close, his hand at her waist and her hand on his shoulder.

And they waltzed.

1-2-3, 1-2-3, 1-2-3

"I guess you're right," mama admitted.

"Of course I am."

He almost stepped on her foot, keeping his arrogance in check. Mama giggled again. She didn't often giggle, which made Mr. Bellamy smile, which made mama smile. A deep smile. That deep smile Rolly had never seen before. A deep smile that made Mr. Bellamy lose his senses for just a second and kiss her.

It was such a fierce kiss, lifting her on her toes, and even deeper than her smile. His arm wound around her waist and his hand cupped her face gently. It was both the most passionate yet tender kiss she'd ever received, and the princess was so swept up, she couldn't think to stop it.

In fact, mama didn't bother stopping it at all.

Mr. Bellamy did.

And quicker than he would have liked, too.

As far as he was concerned, mama was practically engaged to Calvin—whether Calvin was loyal or not, he knew mama was an honest lady. An honest lady who was also his subordinate. All of those misgivings hit him like an anvil, so he let mama go and promptly stepped back.

"I'm..." he cleared the kiss from his throat. "I'm sorry, Miss
Sawyer. My guests..."

"Yes," mama did the same. "They'll be wondering where you
are."

Reaching an understanding, Mr. Bellamy gave her a quick
nod and escaped the office as quickly as he could without tripping
over himself. Mama stayed, though. She stayed and kept soaking in
Lucienne's voice. She'd soon brush off the kiss as a simple accident,
which he couldn't possibly have meant.

But that song.

That song...

It takes me a moment, but I finally realize the French record Hazel
referenced is the exact tune playing on her own record player as we speak.
She closes her eyes, soaking it in as Linda must have. She's starting to sing
the words to the song; she's lost in the memory.

"She sings this all the time," Juliet whispers to me.

"It's a beautiful song," I comment, sneaking another cookie.

Aunt Hazel opens her eyes and smiles widely. "The most beautiful.
Mama never even spoke a lick of French, but she could sing every word of
this song."

the ball

I make a mental note to play this at Aunt Hazel's funeral, if the need soon arises. It is a lovely song, made lovelier by the smile it puts on her face.

the ball

the wizard

Mama was always good at gettin' over stuff. I've said it before. She got over the kiss after a few hours of rationalizing, followed by a good night's sleep. She had bigger things to worry about. Rolly had schoolwork to catch up on. Bills needed paying. The lump of a man still mooching off of her for a free meal. So many things kept her mind off of the kiss that everyone was none the wiser.

As long as they didn't pay attention to Mr. Bellamy.

As long as they didn't really know Mr. Bellamy.

If they didn't really know Mr. Bellamy, they wouldn't notice the way he gazed at her now when she wasn't looking. They wouldn't notice the way he gently touched her arm to get her attention. They wouldn't notice his new eagerness to help her reach a top shelf or steady her on a ladder. They wouldn't notice his softer tone as he spoke to her. They wouldn't notice the new way he worried about her and her kid.

Even mama didn't really notice.

He was always sweeter to mama than anyone else, anyway. He always paid attention—but not like he did after that kiss. There was nothing mentioned, though. Neither of them said a single word. That next Monday in the office, and the week that followed, it was business as usual.

Mama came in, gave Mr. Bellamy his agenda for the day, and recited it aloud. But Mr. Bellamy was only half-listening. He was watching the way mama massaged her hands while she talked.

"Cancel that lunch appointment," he interrupted her. "I made another one."

Mama stopped, eyebrows lifted. "Oh?"

"There's a friend of mine I'd like you to meet."

"What sort of friend?" mama hesitated. She was equal parts hopeful and suspicious.

"He's done a lot of research and trials for the uses of cortisone, recently."

"Cortisone?"

Back then, doctors started giving cortisone shots for things like arthritis and joint pain. It was pretty effective—they still use it. It's a steroid, I think. Either way, mama was surprised. She'd heard of it, but never had the time off to pursue it. Admitting her constant pain to Mr. Bellamy made her anxious; she didn't want him thinking she was incapable of handling the job. Her fears were unfounded, though; his expression read concern, not judgment.

Mr. Bellamy nodded. "Yes. I'd like him to have a look at you. Purely for selfish reasons, of course," he added. "An assistant is much more productive when she's comfortable and out of pain." He flashed a teasing smile at her before turning to the agenda in front of him and continuing their morning routine.

Mama thought about this all morning, with the side of her mouth tugging upward in a small, conflicted smile. She wasn't sure if she liked how much he'd noticed her frequent discomfort, but she couldn't help but be appreciative.

At lunch they met with Dr. George Roland.

"That's my son's name," mama smiled at him as he offered her a chair at their table.

"George?"

"No, Rolland. It's just spelled a little differently." She let Mr. Bellamy scoot her chair in and then take a seat beside her. The two gentlemen picked a quaint, comfortable joint; it was a deli, actually, I think. In any case, they were some of the few customers in the place and chose a secluded corner in which to conduct their business.

"Does he go by Rolly?" the doctor asked curiously. "All the kids growing up called me Roly Poly. It didn't help that I'd roll up on the ground whenever a ball even looked like it was heading in my direction, so the nickname was appropriate, I suppose."

Mama chuckled. "My Rolly is more the type to run toward the ball until it hits him in the face."

Dr. Roland laughed; he was a jolly sort of fellow—slightly round and balding, with tufts of hair on the sides of his head. He wore glasses that sat on the tip of his nose and a fedora on his crown. Rolly called him the Wizard. Politely, he took the hat off and set it on the empty chair beside him, ready to sell his potions.

"So you have yourself a little baseball player, huh?"

"At least he has fun," mama sighed and shrugged. She'd hardly call him a baseball player, but she couldn't deny his enthusiasm for the sport. The number of injuries he'd sustained over those last few years made mama cringe at the thought of him going back outside to play it again. "There's no stopping little boys, is there?"

Dr. Roland angled his head toward Mr. Bellamy and smirked. "Your boy sounds an awful lot like Russell here. Never knows when to quit."

Mr. Bellamy rolled his smirking eyes. "But look where it got me."

"Can't argue with that." The doctor awkwardly paused, intertwining his fingers atop the table between them. His eyes shifted from Mr. Bellamy to mama, unsure where to begin and even more hesitant to cast his assumptions. "You seem awfully young to have the sort of problems he tells me you have," he led.

Mama glanced anxiously at Mr. Bellamy, and then sharply back to the doctor. "Well, what is it he told you I have?"

"Joint pain and fatigue, mostly. But you tell me, sweetheart. How often does this joint pain occur?"

"Um," she hesitated to answer in front of Mr. Bellamy, but when he rested a hand on the back of her chair, for some reason she relaxed just a little bit. "...it's pretty constant."

"Is it worse in the morning?" He reached for a small notebook in his suit pocket.

"Yes."

Jotting some notes, his eyes fixated on the notebook instead of mama, easing mama's mind a little. Less attention on her, you see. "Do you ever feel feverish and weak?"

"Every night."

She could feel Mr. Bellamy shift in his chair. If she had dared glance over again, she would have seen his jaw clench. Had he known the extent of mama's condition he probably wouldn't have worked her so hard. Late hours were hard on her, but mama was the last person to complain.

Dr. Roland pursed his lips up to touch his nose—a funny expression I assume was his contemplative face. Like Mr. Bellamy's mouth-rubbing gesture. He stared at her a moment and then looked as though he wanted to say something to Mr. Bellamy. But he didn't; he instead propped his elbows on the table between them and looked at mama very closely.

"The patients in my trial are considerably older than you, but I think the results should be the same. I've worked it out with Russell —if you're interested, I'd like to administer the shots every couple of months."

Mama massaged her hands, glancing at Mr. Bellamy before answering. "Would it be painful?"

"For the first day or two after the shot, sure. But nothing compared to what you've experienced on a daily basis, I imagine."

"How much would it cost?"

Dr. Roland stared at mama strangely. His stare turned incredulously and shot in Mr. Bellamy's direction. He then lowered his voice toward mama. "I told you, I've worked it out with Russell. There'll be no charge for you, honey."

Mama was in shock for hours after lunch, distracting her late into the evening. Her first official appointment would be at the beginning of the next week. When she got home from work, in time for dinner, it was still on her mind. Mr. Bellamy footed the bill for mama to be out of pain. She knew he was quietly generous by nature —she'd seen enough of his anonymously charitable checks to know his heart was bigger than he pretended—but this was beyond her expectations. Her assumption had been that she was too close to the surface of that big heart that she would only witness the depth of his generosity from a distance.

Calvin was waiting for her on the floor at home, playing a card game with Rolly, and she didn't even sigh in exasperation (like she usually did when she saw him expecting to be fed). Instead, she grinned real big and asked him and Rolly what they'd want for supper. To her pleasant surprise, Miss Hollis was already hard at work preparing a meal. So, leaving the boys to their game, mama helped her.

"Well don't that beat all," Hollis commented after mama told her about her lunch appointment.

"Bizarre, isn't it?" mama leaned with her back against the counter, crossing her arms in front of her chest while Hollis salted the vegetables. "I would've never thought to ask a doctor for cortisone shots."

Hollis scoffed. "When do you have time to sit and think about what to ask a doctor?"

Mama chuckled ironically and dropped her eyes to the floor. "Still, it's awfully nice of him to think of that for me."

Setting the vegetables aside, Miss Hollis raised a suspicious brow at mama, coupled with a sly smile. "Mhm. Awfully nice a-him indeed."

"Awfully nice of who?" Cal appeared in the dining room with Rolly trailing behind him, abandoning their card game.

"Miss Martin says it's *whom*," Rolly corrected. Miss Martin was his new schoolteacher. Funny enough, he hadn't missed a day of school since Miss Martin started at Wilson Elementary.

Calvin just ignored the kid's correction and kept his eyes on mama.

"Mr. Bellamy," she told him. "He got me an appointment with a Dr. Roland."

"For what?"

Mama paused, feeling the side-stare from Miss Hollis bury her. "My pain," mama finally said.

Calvin almost smiled—one of those annoyed, humoring

smiles that suggest the other person is insane. "You mean your headaches?"

"No...my joint pain. Dr. Roland says it's most likely arthritis. He's going to start me on cortisone shots." Mama and Calvin exchanged a conversation with their eyes, one that Miss Hollis could understand but Rolly could not.

"Like some kind of wizard," the boy commented.

"Something like that."

"He has my name, too," he said proudly, sticking his hands in his pockets as Calvin did, as well.

Mama smiled at him, and *only* him. "He does. He said they called him Roly when he was a kid, too. But, he only spells it with one L."

Rolly then shook his head. "Well, then he spells it wrong."

Mama laughed until she caught sight of Calvin's tight face.

"Is he paying for it too?" he pressed.

Standing up straight, now away from the counter, mama tightened her arms in front of her and braced herself. "Yes, he is. Isn't that nice of him?"

Calvin wouldn't cause problems. Not before a meal. He knew better. That's why he waited until supper was finished and Miss Hollis went to clean Rolly up for the night.

I hate this part.

Rolly always hated this part.

He'd heard their fights before, but not like this one.

Calvin meant to propose to mama that night; to lock in their relationship and start their 'forever' together. But hearing Mr. Bellamy's sudden interest in mama's personal life worried him. And when Calvin got worried, he got dangerous. Maybe mama was unfaithful. Maybe Mr. Bellamy figured out Cal's scheme and was trying to stop it by being sweet on mama. It really didn't matter which one was true.

Mama didn't just fall to the floor.

She didn't just cry.

Mama yelped. There was a strangled thud. Dishes shattered. Mama gave a muffled scream and then whimpered. What scared Rolly most was that Calvin didn't shout. He didn't holler and carry on, as he usually did. He was hushed and sinister.

Miss Hollis kept Rolly in the back room, her mouth tighter than a drum. She quickly put him in bed and scurried back to the kitchen. That's when the hollering started. But it still wasn't from Calvin. Miss Hollis shouted louder than Rolly had ever heard—and then a pan hit something hard. He was never sure if Miss Hollis threw one at Calvin or if Cal threw it at her. It didn't make much difference either. He was out of their house in seconds, slamming the front door behind him.

The fear that paralyzed Rolly wore off quickly enough for him to sneak through the hallway and glimpse at the battlefield.

Mama was on the floor, one arm hugging her knees and the other hand gingerly touching her neck. Her cheeks were so wet that even the low-lighting glistened across them. Miss Hollis was crouching in front of her, trying to say something soft to mama.

Mama stopped rubbing her neck and hid her face in her hand. "Did he see?" Tears choked her words.

Miss Hollis didn't give her a straight answer. She didn't even answer right away. She just sat down on the floor beside her and wrapped a motherly arm around her shoulders, kissing the top of her head.

"When he grows up," she murmured softly, "when he grows up and tells stories about his mama....he's not gonna remember seeing you struggle, baby. He's gonna remember seeing you get back up every time you got kicked down."

She was right. She was always so right about mama. And Rolly.

You should have been here to listen to Rolly tell the story. He never spent too much time on mama's failures and weaknesses. He made her into the perfect, strongest, most beautiful princess a story could have. Because that's what she was to him. Mama was perfect.

But this scarred him.

How could someone so perfect be so mistreated?

I guess that's how stories are supposed to go. There's always someone who doesn't see the perfection. Sometimes that someone is the princess herself, sometimes it's the villain. And sometimes it's both. Rolly just never thought he'd see a story where the *prince* would do anything to intentionally hurt the princess.

I would've lost faith in heroes and princes and all that nonsense. The world is full of dragons and trolls. But I'm a cynic. Rolly was a lot of things, but he was never a cynic, not once in his life. Characters in masks didn't break him—they only made him eager to find out what masks all the others wore too.

Aunt Hazel's tears mirror what I imagine fell from mama's own face. She may be a cynic, but she loves her mama. As a child, she probably expected this part all along. Or she had just heard the story so much by now that she couldn't hide her disdain for Calvin Priestley. I think I know now why I'd never heard his name before. For a brief time at the beginning, I suspected he could have been Hazel's father. That theory was pretty quickly dashed, but I didn't expect his part in the story to go this far.

"He should've killed him," Hazel muttered to herself while adjusting the afghan on her lap.

"Rolly was just a child," Juliet pointed out, almost habitually.

I definitely thought she meant Bellamy, but no. Her brother. Little Rolly.

"Doesn't matter," she almost barked. "He should've killed him the first time he touched mama."

"Was that the last time he saw Calvin?" I ask, trying to get her past the well-warranted thoughts of murder.

Like a switch is flipped, she settles and shakes her head distractedly. "No. He saw him twice after that. Both are Rolly's favorite parts, too...one I understand...but why the second, Rolly? I don't understand you sometimes."

Juliet moves to sit directly beside Aunt Hazel, tucking the old woman's short hair behind her ear, bringing her back. "Why don't you tell Keira about the one you understand, first?"

The old woman abruptly looks at her. "Yeah," she gleams. "Yeah, that's up next I think."

the wizard

the duel

It started back at the office again.

The next day, mama did what she did. Picked herself up, dusted herself off, and got back to work, just with a little more makeup this time. Mr. Bellamy didn't suspect a thing, until she leaned over his desk for him to sign a legal document of some kind and he caught a glimpse of the bruise along the side of her neck.

It was hard to miss—shaped like fingers, turning a dark purple. She wore her hair down that day; it was far enough on the back of her neck to be easily hidden by her curtain of curls. But the way she subconsciously tucked her hair out of the way as she leaned over betrayed her, allowing Mr. Bellamy to see.

"What's this?" he shot up from his chair, alarming her.

Mama instantly brushed her hair forward to shield her neck. "What's what?"

"What happened?"

"Nothing," mama put up defenses. "I slept on it funny, and I bruise too easily."

His eyebrows pulled together skeptically. "You slept funny." He wasn't buying it, but mama insisted.

"Yes, I did. I'll have this mailed out this morning," she held up the document he had signed and left the room as swiftly as she could only briefly running into the wall on her way out.

But Russell Bellamy never rolled up on the ground when a ball came at him. He ran toward the ball, even if it hit him in the face. And the older he got, the more likely he was to hit the ball before it met his face.

Just like Rolly. When Rolly was paying attention, he faced the flying ball head-on. He didn't trust Calvin anymore—even felt stupid trusting him from the beginning. But what can a little boy do about it? Well, I'll tell ya....

Rolland Sawyer skipped school.

He played hooky and wandered toward the Bellamy building. He knew Calvin would be leaving work early, because he always did. Calvin Priestley didn't know the meaning of a full day's work. Rolly didn't know what he planned to do, but he knew what he wanted to do. He lingered around the corner of the street nearest the building, noble steed at his side.

Rolly was a good boy. He wasn't the violent sort. He got himself in trouble, but never intentionally like those boys who cause problems and pick fights for no good reason. Murphy sensed Rolly's tension and tried to rub up against his legs to calm him.

"I gotta do something," he muttered to the mutt. "Come on, Murph. What if he does it again?"

Resigned, Murphy sat down and followed Rolly's gaze to the entrance of the Bellamy building, growling under her breath. Sure enough, Calvin exited the building two hours before mama was supposed to. But, to Rolly's surprise, only minutes after him, so did Mr. Bellamy. Rolly saw him smoothly catch up to Cal, grab him by the shoulder, and steer him into the next alley. Hastily clicking his tongue at Murphy, Rolly ran until he was close enough to the impending duel to see.

Dragon versus prince.

The fancy suit fooled everyone.

He was too classy to reduce himself to roughing up men in the streets left and right. And he was intimidating enough that he didn't have to, anyway. In spite of all of that, Mr. Bellamy had Calvin against the wall. He hardly had to touch him, though. His tone was low and menacing. Rolly could hardly understand what he was saying to him, but whatever it was shook the prince to his core. When Cal turned his head away, Mr. Bellamy only slapped it back with sharp force, grabbing his face to keep it focused on those low, menacing words.

Calvin squirmed until he could slink away and disappear across the street. Rolly had never seen him move so fast. Whatever the message was, he understood it—and he had a red, bruising cheek as a reminder. Rolly exhaled too loudly in disappointment, knowing he couldn't run fast enough to catch him, and alerted Mr. Bellamy of his presence in the process.

"Rolland," Bellamy said in surprise, moving toward him. He shoved his hands into the pockets of his pants, clearing his throat with apprehension.

Rolly waved awkwardly at him; Murphy barked her hello. "Hi, Mr. Bellamy. I...um...I was just...I was following the prince...."

"The prince?"

Deeply sighing, Rolly's shoulders slumped. "Yeah. The hero of mama's story. But I don't think....I-I-I didn't know that...."

"Calvin," Bellamy clarified. His eyes wandered away from Rolly and in the direction the coward ran.

"I don't think he is, though. The hero isn't allowed to hurt the princess. I don't think Calvin knew that," Rolly frowned.

Mr. Bellamy crouched a little closer to avoid towering over the boy. "I don't think Calvin was ever meant to be a hero," he assured him.

"Heroes are supposed to fight bad guys and take care of the princess," Rolly kept going.

"That's right," Mr. Bellamy agreed. "At all costs."

"So what does that make Calvin?" Rolly sighed and slipped his hands into his own pockets, leaning back slightly.

Mr. Bellamy paused, trying not to chuckle. "A coward. I think your mother's dealt with enough cowards for one lifetime."

"Is that why you hit him?"

The dragon swallowed hard. Rolly wasn't supposed to see the threats and slaps against the prince. There was enough violence introduced to the Sawyer home, and Mr. Bellamy knew that. He cleared his throat once more. "That? No, that was....that was...well, that was just a bit of chivalry."

"What's that?"

"It's what men do when they're taking care of ladies. They open their doors, offer them chairs, carry their bags...they protect them. Like they're supposed to."

A smile tugged at Rolly's hopeful mouth. "Are you gonna be her hero then?"

"Me?" Bellamy chuckled. "Oh no. She already has a hero."

Rolly didn't know what he meant by that. There were only so many characters in this story. He just assumed Mr. Bellamy was mistaken and went on home. He was a silly boy. Of course mama already had a hero. But in Rolly's eyes, she was also becoming her own. And that's what's important too, I guess.

Mama had become so uneasy in her own home that she started keeping one of the kitchen cleavers by the door. It was a good thing, too, because the same evening Mr. Bellamy confronted him, Calvin decided to pay mama another visit. This time, he didn't make it through the door.

"Who is it?" mama called from the kitchen. He didn't knock —he tried to help himself through the door, but was slowed by the chain lock.

"It's Cal—I wanna talk."

Mama bounded to the door, snatching the cleaver from the hook on the wall as she passed it. Lightly cracking the door open, she held the cleaver in plain view.

"Whoa, put that away!" Calvin's hands shot up at seeing the shine of the blade through the crack. "What's wrong with you? That could kill someone."

"That's the idea," mama told him.

"Hey," he started to lower his hands a little, even stepping forward to see if he could get into the house. If he could get in, he could convince her that he was willing to change. No such luck. Mama held the cleaver higher, with a determined look on her face. "Come on, Linda. I was an idiot, okay? I was afraid of losing you and I overreacted."

"Overreacted?" mama repeated, opening the door wider. The chances of him getting through were unchanged—mama held that cleaver tighter and even closer to his chest. "I could've handled your temper, Cal. I could've. I could've been fine being your doormat—it's in my nature. But I refuse to let you act like that in front of my son."

"Please," Cal completely lowered his hands. "He didn't even see. He was in his room. It was between you and me. I'd never hurt Rolly."

"But you'd hurt me," she reminded him. "You'd hurt me in front of him. And isn't that worse? Poisoning a child, making him believe the hero's not a monster? He deserves better than that." Mama took a shaky breath. "I-I deserve better than that."

"Yes you do, mama," Rolly mumbled from behind her, giving her cause to turn around and providing Calvin the chance to take another step inward.

Mama spun back and pressed the cleaver against Calvin's throat. "Get out," she seethed.

After a lengthy, earnest stare, Calvin finally grunted. "Fine." And he left.

Good riddance.

Mama didn't bother asking why Rolly wasn't ready for bed yet. Instead, she led him back to his room and helped him. He wasn't moving very quickly; his mind seemed preoccupied with more important matters than bedtime. Mama sat on his bed, once she prepared it for him, and watched him diddle daddle. She just smiled at him for a while—not deep or tired, but a relieved smile.

"What is it you're thinking about?" she asked him.

Rolly stopped idly fingering through his dresser and turned to mama. "I know the next part."

"The next part of what?" She lifted her legs up on the bed. "The story?"

He finally found a matching set of pajamas and started changing into them. Before continuing his thought, he buttoned his top and wiggled under the covers next to mama. "Yeah, the story," he went on. "The prince wasn't the prince."

Mama frowned. "No, he wasn't, was he?"

"No, but that's all right." Rolly took mama's hand and held it close.

"Is it?" mama gave a nervous chuckle. "Sometimes the princess is stupid."

Rolly wiggled a little more, his hand beckoning his noble steed into the room and onto the bed. "You're not stupid, mama. And it's okay, anyway; the princess has armor anyway."

"Does she now?"

"Yes, but it doesn't always stop her from getting hurt."

Mama frowned, real hard, and even grunted. "Then what good is it?"

Rolly felt the frown, so he set to fix it. He touched mama's face and pushed a corner of her frown upward, making it into more of a smirk. It was close enough. "It's magic armor. It makes her heal faster and stronger every time she's wounded. So when the prince turns evil and fights her with a sharp sword, or hits her with his shield, the princess is still okay. She just gets back up and slams the door in his face."

Mama chuckled, without nerves this time. "Aggressively slams the door."

"Yeah, and it hits him in the nose and breaks it." Mama laughed and kissed his head, but Rolly was entirely serious, so he went on. "And then, the dragon hunts down the prince and burns him until he's got burn wounds all over his body."

"Wait, what?" She stopped laughing. How could her child have gotten such a graphic idea in his head?

"The dragon burns him. He can breathe fire, you know, mama. It's his favorite weapon. He breathes it in the prince's face, scaring the daylights out of him so he never goes near the castle again."

Mama was silent for a second before she slowly asked, "Did you...did you see the dragon breathe fire?"

"It's all in the name of 'chivary', mama," Rolly sighed.

"*Chivary,* huh?" mama smiled a small smile.

"That's why he didn't kill the prince. If he killed him, the prince wouldn't learn anything at all. The dragon had to teach him a lesson."

Even a dummy could figure out what Rolly saw. Mama knew papa wasn't a violent man; he had a lot of self control, and that's why he was so good at what he did. But, given the right circumstances, papa knew how to intimidate. He once told me about the fight he got into when he was sixteen. The guy had it coming, but all papa did was sock him once in the jaw and walk away. That's all he had to do.

"Wait," I interrupt Hazel. "Bellamy is your dad."

Hazel stares at me like I'm a moron.

I'm not a moron, for the record. I just have enough self control to resist the urge to interrupt her with my theories until now, when they're confirmed. Apparently self control is a family trait, passed down from my great-step-grandpa Russ. I admit, though, I completely forgot Grandpa Russ's last name—I should've put it all together much sooner. I never met the guy. He died before I was born. I guess I just assumed his last name was Sawyer, since that was Grandpa Rolly's name.

"He sure is," she started to grin. "But he wasn't always Rolly's. That's why he always started the story calling him 'Mr. Bellamy'. I didn't see

it coming when I first heard the story either. Granted, I was five years old and wasn't sure what my own last name was. Still....it's a great story."

Her eyes shift past me, reminiscent, and start to glaze over a little.

"When did Rolly start calling him 'papa'?"

Hazel's eyes snap back at me and her mouth tightens, ready to chastise. "Boy, you are an impatient girl, aren't you?"

"Hey," I hold my hands up, "I've been pretty patient so far. I guessed he was your papa a long time ago." My tone is harsh—my own mama is always telling me to watch how I say things, as if I'll learn—but I quickly correct. "It's just such a great story; I can't wait for the next part."

This softens her again. "Yes...it's a great story...and mama's favorite parts are my favorite parts too...the dragon and the princess..."

the duel

the dragon's keep

The only other person papa was chummy with was his cousin. And even he was kept at a distance. Papa wasn't stupid; being too close to a gangster was dangerous, even if you were family. They had a healthy respect for each other, I think, though. I only met Jimmy O'Shea once, but he and papa smiled a lot before shaking hands. Papa would then turn to Rolly and me, with a stern look in his eye, and say "don't you ever talk to Jimmy O'Shea."

According to papa, you protect what's yours, whatever the cost. Even if it meant keeping family at an arm's length. O'Shea was only allowed in the house when papa was home, and even then, he wasn't allowed past the parlor. Mama wasn't to talk to him and neither were we. From what I saw, O'Shea was perfectly fine with that. He usually only visited papa with business anyway.

This started long before I was born, obviously. For as long as mama worked in the Bellamy Building, papa never left her alone with O'Shea—even though O'Shea probably wouldn't have minded. Remember, mama was a pretty little thing. Whenever he visited, he flashed her a wink and a "lovely to see you, Miss Sawyer." Then papa would flash him a glare, roll his eyes, and close his office door behind them.

"Keep an eye on that one," O'Shea would say. But this time he added, "A very close eye."

This time, he'd heard from Mrs. Denning that mama and papa had stopped by papa's manor just outside of town, to pick up some paperwork he'd taken home the other night. And so, O'Shea showed up shortly after they got to papa's home office. Same routine, different office door shutting behind them.

Papa sat behind his desk and proceeded to lean back, in that way he did. "Is that a threat, Jimmy?"

O'Shea didn't sit; he slowly paced the wall nearest the door, glancing around like he was looking for something. He browsed the bookshelves that lined the walls, lightly touched every other volume, and then smirked a little. "I have a few....insights you might find valuable. 'Course that'll depend on the status of our previous negotiation..."

Papa rolled his eyes again. "No negotiation necessary. The offer's been put to rest."

Fully anticipating papa's response, O'Shea shrugged and dramatically sighed. "Very well. It's out of my hands, Russ. There's no telling what Priestley's capable of—he's a reckless fool. A reckless fool you've challenged, apparently."

There was no need to lean back anymore—papa knew exactly what to think. He rested his forearms against his desk and bore intensely into O'Shea's soul. "Priestley's hardly a threat to me."

"No, that's true. You've dealt with him for now," O'Shea turned to pace once more, but not before sending a sly gleam papa's way. "The kid wasn't the only one who saw you getting your hands dirty. I assumed you stepped away from those kinds of...practices—

wealth making you lazy and all that...but I was clearly mistaken."

This was when papa stepped out from behind the desk. O'Shea wasn't as easily intimidated as Calvin was, but that was all just fine—papa moved in close to him in any case, just inches from his face. "You're having me watched." It wasn't a question, it was more like an agitated observation.

O'Shea just gave a hearty chuckle and patted papa on the shoulder. "Paranoid as you are, I expected you to catch on much sooner." He cleared his throat at papa's dark expression. "Don't worry, they've been given strict orders. They won't lay a hand on you. I take care of family—however tiresome they are. My boys *have* been noticing some troubling things about your pretty little assistant, though. She may not be the damsel in distress you've been made to believe she is, my friend."

"Is that right?"

Both eyebrows shot up, and O'Shea snorted lightly. "She got you to hire the Priestley fellow in the first place, didn't she? You don't think she wants your contraband as much as he does? They're practically engaged to be married. What's his is hers...and if she gets him what he wants...what's theirs won't be yours anymore."

Papa thought about this for a moment, stepping away from the threat and sitting back against the edge of his desk. "How long have you been watching Linda?"

"Linda?" O'Shea snorted again, this time rubbing his shaking head in pity for his cousin. "Oh dear. She's good."

"*How long?*"

"Long enough to tell you she'd do just about anything to get out of her current situation. She lives in a dump, hardly sees her kid, and supports Priestley with whatever small wages you pay—"

"They're not small," papa corrected.

"Oh? Well, maybe it all goes to Priestley then. Maybe she's hoarding it for herself—the point is, Priestley's had someone on the inside from the beginning, and you should be wary of her. The idiot thinks doing one little favor for me suddenly makes him my most valuable asset. Really, he's no more than just a convenience. But he wants what he wants—and right now it's what you've got in that vault. That arrogance, Russ, is what'll make him dangerous. And who knows what the girl's planning..."

Papa tightened his mouth and crossed his arms in front of his chest. "You should go, Jimmy."

O'Shea held his hands out expectantly. "What? No compensation for my abundance of goodwill?"

"How valuable is Priestley to you?"

"I've already dismissed him."

"Keep eyes on the Sawyer home, with orders to step in, should Priestley wander that way again....and we'll revisit the loan sharking."

O'Shea grinned. "You're a prince."

"No, I'm not," papa walked him to the door.

Mama was left to her own devices while the two men met in the home office. So she meandered into the various rooms on the first floor. She'd never been beyond the parlor before, so sights like the library and dining room were fascinating. The homes of the rich were a sight to see back then—I suppose they still are.

As Rolly put it, the first time a princess walks through the dragon's keep is always thrilling and mysterious. I grew up there, so the parlors, dining rooms, and hallways aren't all that special, aside from the fact that we all lived in them. But mama lost herself in her tour, until papa found her in the kitchen.

"It's twice the size of mine at home," she told him.

He tucked his hands in his pockets, with no reply. She didn't mind; she simply turned back to the large gas stove she wished she could master. Mama wasn't the greatest cook and always blamed it on lack of practice. When a woman isn't home, she said, she loses touch with the skills that make it a home in the first place.

Finally aware of his eyes still on her, mama turned back to him and asked, "Are we heading back to the office now?"

Papa nodded. "Soon, yes. But first, I have something to show you."

Mama was eager—she hadn't made it to the second floor of the castle yet. To her surprise, though, he took her to the basement

instead. Mama said she was stupid to follow a man into a basement—
she always said only three kinds of men lure women into places alone:
snakes, serial killers, and papa.

But I know papa, and as stupid a decision as it sounds, I can
understand why she trusted him. Papa had safe eyes, even when they
were narrowed and pensive. Those who knew him well could feel very
confident and protected when he looked at them. He was a very good
man. Even so, mama used herself as a cautionary tale.

Don't worry, because it was papa and not a serial killer,
mama wasn't harmed. He only meant to show her the one thing
Calvin had been searching for since he came back into town.

Papa's vault.

The vault was hidden behind a wall which could only be
moved if you lifted the right panel and spun the dial in the right
combination. When the wall moved, there was an even bigger dial
with an even longer combination. Papa opened it effortlessly while
mama's jaw dropped.

Mama had a feeling papa hoarded gold bars, but it was only a
hunch until now. Now that she saw them all, every tall stack covering
almost every inch of the vault, she didn't know what to say. Toward
the front were velvety black boxes, filled with priceless jewelry. Papa
even opened one so she could see the beautiful necklace inside.

"Why are you showing me this?" she asked.

"Have you never received one?"

Mama's face went vacant, staring at the necklace. "My husband never gave me anything but a son." Her eyes grew wide, soaking in the gleam of the small jewels. It was the prettiest thing she had ever seen.

Hazel pauses for a moment, getting up from her armchair and leaving the room.

"Where's she going?" I whisper to Juliet.

She only shrugs and watches for the old lady to return. When Hazel shuffles back in, I notice she's now holding a black velvety jewelry case between her hands. Slowly she makes her way back to her chair, caressing the top of the case of what I assumed was Linda's necklace. The look in her eye is distant, but soft. She has a light smile, as if remembering her mama wearing it around her dainty neck. She opens the case to show me the simple, but glorious necklace.

"It was just her size too," Hazel chuckles. "She let me wear it on my wedding day...no one had given her anything like it."

"Not even Priestley?" papa asked.

At the mention of his name, mama looked away and shook her head. The name upset her, but she couldn't let him see. Guilt and regret set in; mama hated Calvin. But she knew she used to tell herself she loved and needed him. And for that she felt downright foolish.

"You shouldn't show this to people," mama said, shutting the case for him.

"I know," he placed the necklace back in the vault, turning to seal it all in place. "There are men who would kill to get their hands on it. That's why I'm not showing it to people," he turned back to mama, "I'm showing it to you."

Mama still couldn't look at him. She focused her attention on her hands, massaging them lightly as always. "You hit him," she muttered. She didn't need to say his name and papa didn't need to hear it again to know exactly who she meant.

"Is that what Rolland said?" he assumed.

Mama smiled just a little. "He said the dragon breathed fire and burned the prince. Apparently he had to teach him a thing or two about 'chivary'."

Rolly called it that for the rest of his life, and papa would just look on, smiling proudly at him while he said it. So you can imagine how papa chuckled at hearing mama quote him too. The chuckle faded rather quickly, though, when papa remembered why Calvin needed to learn 'chivary' in the first place. He shouldn't have laid a hand on mama, and now they both knew that.

"You weren't at fault," papa said, his voice low. They hadn't talked about her bruises since that first day he saw them, but papa knew exactly why Calvin gave them to her. It was that darn, haunting kiss. "The fault was mine and I'm sorry."

141

"It's all right," mama shrugged. It wasn't, but she'd already dusted it off anyway. Or at least tried to. "It was an accident; you didn't mean it." She finally looked up at his face. "Besides, he didn't care about losing me....maybe only a little...he was more worried that I would go weak at the knees and confess to you the entire plan. I should've warned you..."

"You would've stolen from me?" He thought he knew the answer—mama didn't have a deceitful bone in her body.

"Probably, before..." she surprised him. "If he had wanted me to...and I'm silly that way." Mama looked at her hands again, smiling a little in spite of herself.

"That is silly," papa murmured. When mama looked back up at him, he was smiling. "I would just give you whatever you asked, you know."

Mama didn't know that—though she should've. He hired Calvin, after all. Papa was no fool. He knew the sort of slime Cal was, but after hearing mama say she loved the man, he couldn't say no to her. Even at the cost of his own business. Of course, papa would've never let Calvin get that far in his plan. Like I said, papa was no fool. He just loved mama. But if love makes us fools, then I guess papa, in some respect, was the biggest fool there was.

"I can sense a swindler a mile away, Miss Sawyer," he assured her. "I didn't give him a chance because I trusted him. I gave him a chance because you asked me to." See, I told you as much. "I'm sorry he wasn't what you deserved."

Mama was desperate, but she wasn't stupid either. She knew all along Calvin wasn't what she deserved. Sometimes women like her have a hard time admitting that, though, because they don't believe happy endings are meant for them. They only believe in mediocre endings.

She just shrugged, pretending she didn't mind. "I was a means to an end," she explained. "I can't hate him too much. In a sense, he was a means to an end too..."

"To what end?"

Mama's hands stopped massaging themselves and hid behind her crossed arms in front of her chest. She held them tightly, feeling the sadness of her truth come out. "He said he would marry me. He said he would get a big fortune and take me away from here. He said...he would save me." Her hands now out of the way, mama glanced down at her feet as she sighed, "I needed him."

"No, you didn't," papa said in that cold, matter-of-fact way he said things. Mama's glance moved back up to him, desperately waiting for an explanation. "You didn't know what you needed. You were doing just fine without him. You have a son—"

"Yes," mama snapped, unexpectedly. "A son who needs a mother and a roof over his head and I can't properly give him both."

Papa sighed at her defensive stance. "You're a wonderful mother. You love Rolland and he has everything he needs; you support him the best way you possibly can."

Tears welled up in mama's eyes, but she fought them back into mist. "But I hate it," she said.

"Of course you do; your boss is absolutely hateful."

This succeeded in making mama smile again, even laugh, which is what papa wanted.

"I'm sorry. I shouldn't complain so much," she corrected herself.

This time papa laughed. "I think you've earned the right to," he told her. As if suddenly remembering they were alone, and in a basement, papa gently placed a guiding hand on her back and led her up the stairs while he continued. "But it isn't an escape plan you need."

"Then what do I need?" she humored him, letting him take her back toward the parlor. When they got there, he stopped in front of her and faced her squarely, with a tender look about him.

"Are you happy, Linda?"

It alarmed her a little to hear him say her first name, but not as much as it alarmed her to think of a question like that. No one had ever asked her if she was happy before. She had never given it a single thought. At home it was Rolly's happiness, and at work it was Mr. Bellamy's.

"I-I don't know," was all she could think to say.

Papa nodded, knowing that would be her answer. "I think

that's what you need."

"To know?"

"To be happy."

the dragon's keep

the wish

Calvin stopped showing up to work, but that was no surprise. Don't think he's gone forever—I made that mistake—because he'll be back. Thankfully, though, it takes him a good long while. He had other plans to occupy his time. Mama was relieved, and papa hardly cared. He didn't do much more than occasionally run an errand for Mrs. Denning anyway. Anyone could do that.

It was a couple of weeks after papa showed mama the vault. Things weren't quite business-as-usual as they pretended to be after the kiss, but they tried. Mama smiled a little more. Papa made more jokes. Mama told funny stories of Rolly more often. Papa asked how the kid and the dog were doing.

Mrs. Denning started paying attention now. And it worried her a little. She liked papa well enough, but she knew mama wasn't always careful. She mentioned once to papa that it was a hard world for naive young ladies who work around influential, powerful men. They're easily manipulated, she told him, especially when they're most vulnerable. *Prey*, she called them. And the powerful men, their predators.

She was only taking care of mama. Looking out for her, when she thought she couldn't look after herself. And Mrs. Denning knew what happened with Calvin, so she was afraid mama was too desperately seeking comfort and protection.

Papa knew that, and he hadn't considered how this new attention might come across—to mama and to everyone else. So he got careful. He didn't stand so close, he made mama go home earlier every night while he finished up their work alone, and he only talked about her personal life if she initiated the conversation.

Mama didn't mind—not that she noticed too much of a difference. She was too busy noticing her own happiness. Earlier nights meant more outings with Rolly. No Calvin meant more money to save and spend on Rolly. She was starting to smile more on her own now, and it was beautiful. So beautiful that papa kept finding it harder to keep his distance. But he did his best.

After a short while, O'Shea sent papa a message that said his boys noticed Calvin and another guy hanging around the streets where mama and Rolly lived. O'Shea thought they could've followed her home from work once or twice too. To test this, papa decided to keep mama a little later again. While she dictated an amendment to some contract they were working on, papa lingered near his office window, glancing down every now and then at the street below. Sure enough, he caught a glimpse of Calvin's dark blonde head stepping in and out of the shadows.

He was waiting for mama.

"That's enough for today," papa said. He cleared his throat, took his coat off its stand and grabbed his briefcase. "I'll be taking you home now, Miss Sawyer."

Mama's hand froze and she dropped her pencil on the desk. "Oh, you will?"

"It's a cold night," he confirmed, gesturing to the window. "And there's no sense hailing a cab when my car is available."

Suspicious, mama went to the window where he gestured and glanced to see what could've caused the abruptness. That's when she saw Calvin and her hands tightened into small fists. She brought one up to subconsciously rub her neck. "Y-yes, it is..." she tried not to stammer. "Thank you, sir."

He guided her out of the office and to the parking garage, muttering a quiet, "only a lift," to Mrs. Denning as they passed her desk. But it wasn't only a lift—Rolly made sure of that. It was dinner and a story.

Rolly's favorite parts were the ones with the dragon. He told me that over and over again, even after I knew who the dragon really was: my papa. He claimed that dragons are exciting and powerful and wondrous creatures. He said everybody should have a dragon. Made them sound like pets. But they're not. They're big and imposing and would break everything in the house. I told him this and he'd tug at my hair, as if I was wrong.

Apparently I was missing the metaphor. I was only nine before I learned to stop arguing with a big brother who was right all the time.

Rolly would assure everyone that dragons are not pets. In this part of the story he would say they were "well-mannered house guests." Papa would laugh and say "all the best dragons have excellent manners." Rolly would agree, shoot me a glare and say "see, I told you so."

I definitely missed the metaphor, but papa was much gentler in explaining that to me. He was always gentle with me, just as he was with mama.

He and Rolly spoke a different language with one another. Rolly liked to impress him and papa liked seeing how great Rolly could be. He corrected him—sternly, too—but cheered the loudest when the kid did good. They were like this from the beginning. Which is why Rolly wouldn't let papa simply give mama a ride home from work. He grabbed his hand, dragged him into the house, and told mama that he was staying for dinner.

Anxious as mama was about cooking for Mr. Bellamy, Rolly's excitement at the dinner guest wasn't dampening. She didn't dare spoil it—not after Calvin. It may not have been Rolly who got the bruises, but mama was afraid of what the ordeal would do to his development. She worried about that for years. Young boys are impressionable. Mama even got tense when Rolly raised his voice—which he rarely did. Heaven forbid he pick up on Calvin's bad habits.

So to the kitchen mama went, pretending it was no trouble, while Rolly sat with papa in the living room and impressed him with his skills with that silly toy gun. It was Miss Hollis's day off, but she had stopped by to pick up some baking flour mama promised her.

She saw mama's tight face trying to focus on the ingredients in her cupboard.

"Need help, sugar?"

Mama hardly noticed she was there and absently replied, "The sugar's with the flour if you want some of that too."

Miss Hollis laughed warmly. "No, no, honey. I meant you. Do you need some help?"

Mama turned to her desperately and leaned all of her weight into the counter behind her, gripping the corners for dear life. "On your day off?" mama said first. She didn't want to impose on another woman's day of freedom, but she secretly hoped Miss Hollis would push and insist on helping anyway.

Which she did.

"Oh, sweetheart, you give me enough a-those. What kinda supper you think Mr. Bellamy would like?" she whispered. She set down her flour and tied her apron, which hung up on the wall, around her waist.

Mama sighed. "I can't even begin to guess."

Miss Hollis laughed again, but quieter this time. "My, he sure has you flushed, miss."

It wasn't a hard thing, making mama flushed. Her face went red when she was laughing, crying, angry, sad, embarrassed— everything. But in this case, Miss Hollis' instincts were reliable. Mama never thought too much of it, but she was never this nervous when whipping up a soup or sandwich for Calvin.

Papa's taken too good a care of her for him to have a disappointing meal in her home. It was unacceptable. No one cares about that stuff anymore, but in those days, a woman's skill in the kitchen was viewed a little differently. And I've already said how mama had very little. Her cooking was edible, but not savory.

Lucky for mama, we had Miss Hollis.

Without another word, she quickly put together the most delicious chicken dinner. The three of them devoured it, while Miss Hollis quietly snuck away. Rolly bragged about how good mama was at making him food—of course his standards were based on her ability to make him a bowl of breakfast cereal.

Regardless, papa smiled and acknowledged how skilled mama was, which made her smile. She liked the praise and thought she had him fooled. Until, of course, he winked at her and quietly said,

"Thank Miss Hollis for me, as well. It was delicious."

Mama blushed again, but his grin remained. It made no difference to him who made it. Food was food, he always said. Living as long as he did before marrying mama, he was used to eating other people's food. He had a house cook, but he frequented restaurants more than his own dining room table.

His smile kept mama smiling through the rest of the meal. Rolly went on and on about Murphy and all the tricks she knows. He chattered as if he'd known papa all his life, and he was determined to report on everything he could.

When supper came to a close, mama cleared the table while the boys talked, then tried to serve papa coffee the way she did when they were in the office. The moment Rolly's chatter came to a natural stopping point, papa stood and stopped her.

"You're off the clock, Miss Sawyer," he said, taking the coffee pot out of her hands. "Allow me." And he took a turn pouring the cups, letting mama sit and listen to the rest of Rolly's riveting account of the time Murphy stole butcher's scraps and was chased down the street with a meat cleaver.

After Rolly said "the end" and waited for the applause and praise of his eager audience, it was time for bed. Papa insisted on cleaning up while mama put Rolly to bed. In this day and age, it's no big surprise when a man cleans the kitchen—well, at least, not as much as it used to be. Mama was nearly speechless at such an offer, and almost didn't allow it, until Rolly dragged her away to finish their bedtime routine and continue their story.

"Okay, now," mama settled into the bed once again. "Where did we leave off?"

Rolly thought for a moment. "Um, the evil prince got burned by the dragon."

"Oh yes, that's right. Do you think the prince came back?"

"Well, sure he did. He probably came back with other

soldiers."

"You're right. He got all the mean villagers together to fight the dragon."

"They don't know he's good, do they," Rolly lowered his voice like it was a secret.

Mama shook her head. "No, they don't know he's good. They don't realize he's only protecting the princess." She paused for a moment of realization. "The evil prince doesn't care though. He only wants to hurt other people and steal the dragon's gold—no matter what it takes."

"Is the dragon a prince?"

"What do you mean?"

Rolly cleared his throat, as he had heard papa do, before explaining himself. "The evil prince can't be the prince, because heroes don't hurt princesses. So does that mean the dragon is a prince who was cursed and now the princess has to break the curse so he can be a person again?"

Mama squinted as she considered this. "I don't think the dragon was cursed. He doesn't strike me as the sort of dragon who would do anything he didn't want to do. I think he might pretend to be a dragon....It's much easier to scare people and keep them away when you look like a dragon, you know. I'm sure when he's safe in his cave, he's probably a nice prince again."

"It's a castle, mama," he chided. "He doesn't live in a cave—he lives in a grand castle."

"But of course, forgive me."

"I bet you he only turns into a prince in front of the princess because she's his true love and she could break the curse."

"There's no curse, Rolly."

"Oh that's right."

"And we don't know that the dragon has a true love," she shifted uncomfortably.

"Sure he does. So does the princess. I wish it was each other. I think that'd be nice, if you like that kind of story. I wish it was, because ladies always like those kinds of stories—with happy ever afters and all that. And you're a lady, mama."

"Well," she sprung smoothly from the bed and made for the light switch. "I think that's a good place to end for the night, don't you think?"

"It's true though, isn't it, mama? And a wish can make any story true."

"No, sweetheart. Real life is a little different. And this...this is just like any old story." She flipped the switch and heard him say softly through the darkness,

"But, mama, your story's not old. It's still brand new. So I'll keep wishing."

Mama's house wasn't big. Sound carried. Rolly heard every

fight she had with Calvin, every complaint Miss Hollis had about the neighbors, and every grunt of pain mama made before pulling herself into bed. Sure enough, papa could hear small pieces of that story as Rolly's voice lifted at the thought of the dragon. Papa was familiar with it—Rolly was sure to tell him while they waited on dinner.

Mama returned to the kitchen to relieve papa of dish duty after offering him another piece of leftover tarts. Papa insisted on finishing the last dish before eating the tart over the sink, taking care not to dirty another dish for mama to clean.

"Rolland's story," he began after swallowing. "About the princess and the dragon..."

"It's just a story," mama said quickly, afraid he heard too much of it.

"But it's yours," he pointed out.

"Yeah, I guess so."

He chewed and swallowed his last bite. "How does it end?"

Mama put the rest of the tarts back in the cupboard, avoiding direct eye contact. "You mean, who wins? The prince or the dragon?"

"The princess wins," he stated simply, watching her reach to place the tray in its spot. "That's not what I'm asking. I'm asking how she wins. How does she beat the evil prince?"

She spun around, a little surprised at the concept. *The princess wins.* She liked the sound of that. "Um, she befriends the dragon," she finally answered. "He helps her."

"That's awfully nice of him," he smirked to himself, giving the counter one more wipe for crumbs, for good measure.

Mama smirked too. She dared inch closer to him, leaning against the same counter. "Yes...he didn't turn out so bad after all."

"I'm sure the princess brought out the best in him." He lowered his tone, enough for her to move in closer to respond in kind.

"Oh, I don't know," she said, now only inches away. "I think she finally took a moment to see the best in him that was already there."

"Linda," he whispered, so Rolly couldn't hear. "The burned prince returning with villagers may be more than just a fairytale."

"What does that mean?" She knew what it meant. Sometimes ladies pretend they don't know any better, just to hear how much men worry about them.

"Priestley's schemes may continue," he warned her, "whether you're a part of them or not. I need you to be careful."

Mama couldn't help but give a deep smile, one of those rare ones that were becoming more and more common. "I will be," she promised. "I have the bedtime prince in there, and his noble steed, to keep me safe." Then, matching his whisper, she added, "And there's a dragon looking after me too."

Papa couldn't dislike her tone, or what she tried to do next.

But all he could remember was Mrs. Denning warning him about the harm that could come to mama if he became a predator. So, he surprised them both when mama lifted herself up on her toes to kiss him: he stopped her.

"Linda," he sighed, holding both of her shoulders away from him. He hated himself for it, but he couldn't allow it. Seeing the hurt and confusion in mama's eyes, his jaw clenched. "I—"

"No, no, it's all right," mama lied. She backed away hastily, even brushing the embarrassment off on her skirt.

"No, it isn't. I've...I've been...trying to be as harmless as I possibly can be..."

"*Harmless...*" mama almost chuckled the word. She always thought she was weak, but she never imagined she'd need to be handled with such kid gloves.

"Linda," he stepped toward her, and mama stepped back. "You've been victimized enough—I didn't want to seem..."

"Seem like what?" she almost accused.

Papa sighed with regret again; mama was growing defensive and, now that she'd felt her little bit of happiness, she wasn't ready to be pushed around again. "A predator," he exhaled.

Mama laughed without humor, nodding like the idiot she felt she was. "Of course. Of course, you should...you should save face." Straightening her back and dusting her hands on the bottom of her blouse, mama was ready to get back to work. "I understand."

"Linda, I never meant—"

"I'll be fine, sir," she said. He cringed that she'd reverted back to calling him *sir*. "I always am."

Mama put on another smile, but it sure wasn't deep. Papa never forgot that smile. It was the kind you only give when you've given up on something you've really wanted in exchange for something less. Mama found her happiness in Rolly. That made the smile enough for her. But the princess finally thought she loved that dragon, and it turned out he didn't want her.

It was just as well, she told herself. Princes historically had to be careful who they loved and wed. And if Rolly was right, and the dragon was a shape-shifting prince, then the dragon prince had to be even more careful. For he had the grandest castle in all the kingdoms. How would that look? What would the townspeople say? A majestic dragon prince married to a pitiful princess from a lower kingdom?

Everyone thought Miss Hollis went home to enjoy the rest of her night off, but after supper was cooked she only went home to drop off her flour. She came right back to make sure the night went well. She was so quiet that mama didn't hear her sneak back in, nor did she hear her hide in the pantry during the humiliating rejection.

"You all right, honey?"

Startled, mama's tears leaked. "Yes," she answered too quickly.

Miss Hollis came out of hiding and approached mama slowly. "Are ya sure, there?"

More tears leaked and mama sniffled. "I'm not stupid," she defended.

"I know you're not."

"You think I am, sometimes...but I-I'm not stupid," mama whimpered, biting her lip in a vain attempt to stop crying. She massaged her hands again, less to relieve the pain and more for the comfort it tried to bring.

"I know, baby girl." Miss Hollis pulled mama in close and held her while she cried.

Papa hated this part of the story. For him, I think, this is the most painful chapter. Even counting what happens later. He couldn't stand seeing mama hurt—and he definitely couldn't stand being the one to hurt her. When he left her house that night, his jaw was clenched so tightly it ached. Just like mama's heart. While he drove home she stood alone in the kitchen, biting her lip until the tears stopped spilling.

She was strong now, though she didn't feel it.

She was happy now, though she forgot it.

It wasn't all right. Her smile wasn't deep enough yet.

the wish

the
happy ever after

the happy ever after

Mama was never bothered by that part, but I agree with papa. Seeing mama sad is my least favorite part of the story. Unfortunately, she was sad a lot at the beginning, but nothing compared to how sad she was when she thought she was about to be the happiest she could have been. Mama never minded though, because whenever she helped Rolly tell this story, she always knew it would get better.

That was just mama.

She was the queen of "it would get better." And that's why Rolly was the way he was. It would always get better. Just pick yourself up, dust yourself off, and get back to work. It'll all work out one way or another as long as you just keep going.

Papa and I were different people. We didn't like leaving things to fate. Things only worked out if you made them work out. If they didn't work, it means you failed and needed to keep working at it. I guess that's why this part makes so much sense to me.

Mama kept going. She went back to work, wore that sad smile, and moved forward the best way she knew how. But papa wasn't happy with that. Their interactions went cold. The professionalism came back even stronger than before. She was full of "yes, sir" and "no, sir." And he was expected to go back to calling her "Miss Sawyer." It was excruciating, for both of them. But mama accepted it.

the happy ever after

She had even thumbed through the local papers for other jobs in other offices. It turned out she had been extremely lucky to get the position she had with the Bellamy Company. The competition out there was stiff and filled with men more qualified than she was. The workforce was even tougher back then than it is now.

Papa noticed the classified section of the paper laying out on mama's desk. And if he hadn't noticed it, Mrs. Denning would've told him. She was even more afraid of losing mama than he was. No one else would hire her—remember, she wasn't the best around, or even close to it, and she was well aware.

Mama took an extended lunch break to meet a gentleman for a job interview. She'd never tell papa that, of course. She only told him she had an appointment, but he knew better. So did Mrs. Denning. She sat at her desk, tapping her foot so anxiously that papa almost came out of his office to tell her to stop.

He stood to do so, but was stopped by the sight of little Rolly strolling through the offices. No mama, no Murphy, just Rolly. He was a young man on a mission, wearing the most determined expression papa had ever seen on his face before or since.

Rolly approached Mrs. Denning's desk and cleared his throat politely, the way papa does. "Excuse me, Mrs. Denning," he said.

She was a little surprised to see him, but in amused awe at his manners. Dragons always have excellent manners, remember.

"Why yes, Mr. Sawyer? Your mother's out to lunch, you know."

"I'm not here for mama," he told her succinctly, like the little professional he was pretending to be. "I'm here to meet with Mr. Bellamy."

Papa was already standing in the doorway so Mrs. Denning waved Rolly on in. Humoring him with a smirk on his face, papa shut the door behind them and told Rolly to take a seat in front of his desk.

"What can I do for you today?" papa took his own seat behind the desk, leaning back in his chair.

"I thought the dragon was going to save the princess," Rolly posed, in the most solemn tone to ever escape his lips.

Papa stared at him for a moment before mustering a response. "It's just a story, Rolland," he replied gingerly.

Rolly wasn't satisfied. "It's mama's story." He straightened his back, ready to negotiate. "The dragon is supposed to save the princess, sir. If the prince is evil, he can't do it. She needs the dragon."

"I told you..." papa started impatiently, but then softened his tone. He pressed his arms against the edge of his desk, lowering his head. "I told you, I'm not her hero. She already has one."

"But she's only a little happy with me."

"She loves you, Rolland."

A little shocked at the assumption, Rolly stopped mid-syllable. "I know that. I didn't say mama didn't love me. But you give her a deep smile."

"A deep smile," papa repeated.

"Yeah...she smiles at me all the time. But mama hurts, so her smile is small. She tries so hard, sir. But you make her give deep smiles, like when Miss Hollis snuck and made us chicken. Mama said deep smiles make her forget the pain. Deep smiles and listening to my stories, she says. I can keep telling her stories, sir, but the princess has to be happy with deep smiles or this story can never be finished. And I'd really like to start another one, if you don't mind, sir."

Papa listened intently to the boy's plea. It wasn't anything he hadn't already been thinking about from the moment he left mama's house, the night when Miss Hollis snuck and made the chicken. He leaned back again as Rolly spoke. The kid's hands were tucked firmly in his own pockets and his back straightened confidently.

"All right, Rolland. What would you like me to do?"

Rolly was gone by the time mama got back from lunch. Her interview didn't go well, but she didn't mind. She didn't like the look of the guy anyway. He wasn't anything like papa, and it didn't feel right. Walking back to her desk, she wondered if she should just stay where she was and pray the coldness passes. Awkward as it was, the Bellamy Company was her best chance. The classified pages were getting slimmer and slimmer, with less options every day.

"Miss Sawyer," papa emerged from his office. He beckoned her inside and for a moment mama panicked that he might have seen her job search.

When they were both seated papa cleared his throat. "I understand you're looking for work."

Now the panic resurfaced. Mama scooted to the edge of her chair, and with a deeply apologetic tone she held up a hand she said, "I was only looking. I would never just leave without securing you a replacement, sir."

"Then you'll have to start," he said plainly.

"I'm sorry?"

"Find yourself a replacement, Miss Sawyer." His clarification did nothing to soften the blow.

Mama stared with her mouth hanging open. "But, sir, I—"

"In a timely fashion, if possible."

"You're...y-you're letting me go?"

Clearing his throat again, papa rose from his chair and paced in the direction of his bookshelves just near the phonograph. His hands shoved deep in his pockets, he began. "I tried so desperately to remain honorable and above board. You've made it more and more difficult, Miss Sawyer."

"I'm sorry," she mumbled. She wasn't sure why she was sorry, but she certainly felt she should be, whatever the reason.

Papa turned slowly on his heel. "You..." he started, then stopped. Exhaling, he started to pace again.

"If I've done something wrong, sir, I'm sorry." Mama had leapt to her feet, stepping forward to plead in sincerity. "It won't happen again. And if this has anything to do with last week—I'm ashamed of it and I can move past it. I won't let anything like that—"

"Linda," he snapped at her. He didn't mean to sound so cross; his nerves were getting the better of him. Papa told Rolly that in confidence; so, of course Rolly told me in his own retelling of the tale. Papa had nerves, and just like any man, sometimes that made him snappish. "I've failed to remain detached....failed miserably. And it isn't fair to you."

"What?" she breathed.

"I can no longer have you working here," he sighed, bracing himself for the next sentence. "Because I refuse to employ my wife in an office all day when she'd rather be elsewhere."

Papa liked to tease mama when he was trying to forget how nervous he was; the way she froze like a statue and her eyes grew like a terrified deer in the middle of the road. He'd imitate her confusion, laugh, and then kiss her head like it was all the most adorable thing. He couldn't figure out if she was confused or terrified. Mama always patted his face in scolding and insisted she was only confused—why would she be terrified of the thing she wanted most? Because she finally got it, papa would say.

In the moment, though, I don't think papa was much in the mood for teasing her. Her long pause made him more nervous, but she couldn't gather the words to respond.

"I-I...what...you're...are you...why?" was all that came out.

And that's when papa grabbed mama and kissed her. It was just as impassioned as the first time—or maybe more so. But thankfully for both of them, there was no cutting it short. It wasn't an accident this time, and it wasn't going to be a secret mistake. It was going to be the start of everyone's lives.

When their lips separated, mama asked him, "What made you think I'd say yes?"

"A little optimism I may have picked up from your boy," and papa kissed her again, lifting her chin just a little.

"And you're sure you want me?" mama double-checked.

Papa laughed and kissed her forehead. "Yes, I'm sure."

"Why?"

"Because, contrary to Rolland's stories, sometimes the princess saves the dragon," he kissed her one more time. "And if the dragon sheds a few of his prideful scales, he could actually let her."

the happy ever after

"I knew it would end up happy," I applaud. "Mama got her deep smile."

But Aunt Hazel is not smiling.

"I'm not finished yet, Keira. Rolly never ended the story there, like he should have."

Juliet rises to get us all some water, like she knows what's next. Hazel massages her hands like mama and takes a few short breaths. None of them quite do the trick, so she settles on a big deep one.

"We haven't gotten to his other favorite part," she mutters. "I'll never understand why he loved it so much. Mama always left the room when he told it. It just...it hurt too much."

Oh no. I don't like the sound of that. I predicted the love, the proposal, the happy ever after. What could be left? What more is there?

Ominously, Aunt Hazel shifts in her seat, takes a sip of water, and tightens her mouth before approaching the end.

the happy ever after

the end

the end

I told you Rolly had two favorite parts of the story, and I never understood either of them. The first was when papa fought Calvin in the alley. The second...I understand even less.

The Wizard's cortisone shots worked their magic. She got two in one month, which was more than normal, but her wedding anxiety aggravated her joint pain. Mama was feeling great on the outside, and she was over the moon on the inside.

It was a beautiful wedding, though. Worth the nerves and the cortisone. Rolly said it was like a fairytale. Mama looked like a princess in her silky white dress and her long veil. Walking down the aisle of that little church, mama was an angel. And papa stood waiting for her at the altar, like the handsome dragon prince he was. They said their "I dos" and had the most romantic kiss you could ask for in a wedding. At least, that's what Rolly said. Men usually aren't the best judge of those kinds of things, but mama agreed with him so I suppose he could have been right.

It was mama's happy ever after.

When the wedding was over and real life came back, mama found her replacement as papa's assistant—he was a young man she met at Dr. Roland's office. He couldn't have been more than nineteen when he started. He wanted to be in business, you see, so mama thought who better a study than papa for a young budding businessman. Carl, I think his name was. Little Carl was with papa for years after mama trained him. Papa promoted him to partner when Rolly turned it down. Rolly wasn't much for business—he would've rather been out catching bad guys.

Especially after the bad guys caught him.

If Murphy had been allowed in that bank, Rolly swore the two of them could have stopped it all from happening.

But she wasn't there.

It was just him and mama.

With her wedding certificate tight in hand, mama took Rolly to the bank during lunch—she was still working with papa, training Carl—so she could change her last name on her account. She and papa kept most of their money in that vault he had in the house, but there were still advantages to using banks, even in those days when no one trusted them. Papa was a businessman, after all. "Don't keep all the eggs in one basket," he'd say.

This time of day the bank wasn't the busiest mama had seen it. She had run errands for papa to the bank before and she couldn't remember ever seeing so few people there. Aside from the tellers, there were probably only a few other folks there dealing with their money affairs.

Rolly had never been in a bank before so he didn't stay too close to mama once they were inside. He explored here and there,

the end

eventually circling back to the counter where mama was signing papers and showing her certificate. He almost ran into a man who looked a little familiar to him, but he side-stepped him while the man took a lean against one of the counters. His hat was pulled down over the top of his face, and he didn't lift his head to talk.

The way Rolly describes it, the doors flung open, but mama insists it was much quieter than that. Gangsters were big back then— barging in waving their Tommy guns in the air with stray bullets flying. But these were no gangsters. Not real ones, anyway. They didn't have Tommy guns. They had little revolvers they hid in their coats until they decided there were few enough witnesses for them to strike.

There were four of them. A tall one, a fat one, a Spanish one, and their short leader.

Calvin.

The minute the guns were pulled from behind their coats the remaining customers ducked as close to the counters as possible. Mama nearly smashed her marriage certificate in her hand as she dropped to the floor, panicking when she couldn't see Rolly. He was on the other side of the room, trying to figure out how he recognized the man in the hat.

Calvin shouted above the screams for the tellers to hand over as much of the cash as they could get their hands on. He pointed his gun with a little more precision than the other three, moving it from one teller to another. Their fear was evident, and they all acted quickly to obey his orders.

Hearing his voice struck mama in the face. She was stronger now, remember. Stronger and happier, and she was not going to let Calvin take that away again.

So mama stood up.

She was done cowering, done hiding, and done being afraid of him.

She straightened her back, despite the teller closest to her gesturing violently for her to return to the floor for her own safety. "Rolly!" she called out, holding her breath until she saw Rolly's little head peer out from behind the man in the hat.

"Mama," Rolly replied, much quieter. As if dodging bullets that hadn't yet been fired, he darted across the way, aiming to hold tightly to mama's legs.

But Calvin stopped him.

Cal didn't know mama would be there. He certainly didn't know Rolly would be there. His precision faltered a little when he heard the name and saw the boy. Instinctively, he aimed the gun in Rolly's direction.

"Rolly, stop!" he yelled.

The kid froze. His eyes were wide, but he was too stubborn

the end

to raise his hands, no matter how scared he was. "Cal..." he uttered.

If there was any moment for Calvin to seek redemption, this probably would've been it. If he had been a better man he would've seen Rolly's disappointment in him, taken it to heart, and changed his ways. Rolly's opinion has that effect on a lot of people, me included. But Calvin was a survivor. An opportunist. A scoundrel.

And no one can help someone who won't change. Not even Rolly.

"Cal, I'm a better shot now," Rolly told him.

For a second, it was as if there wasn't a gun pointed at him. He saw the prince he grew up playing baseball with, having adventures, and learning to shoot a toy gun properly. One of the few times mama sat through this part of the story, she mentioned Calvin tearing up just a little when Rolly tried to make him proud.

But monster's only cry empty tears. Or scared ones.

Calvin stepped forward with the gun, trying to prompt Rolly to stick his hands in the air. "Mine's real this time, pal. Watch your step."

Rolly stared at him in confusion. "But, you wouldn't hurt me."

"No, he won't, sweetheart," mama said, moving tensely toward them.

Feeling her edge closer, Cal put the gun on mama instead.

178

the end

"Don't press your luck, Linda," he warned her. "This isn't about you and the kid."

The Spanish robber sighed dramatically, grabbing bags of cash from the teller. "Come on, Priestley," he grunted. "Someone will notice and send the police this way."

Unlike Rolly's, mama's hands lifted in defense. "Take your cash, Cal," she said.

He scoffed like she was joking. "Well it's all I got now, isn't it? Not all of us can live a life of luxury with Mr. Golden Bricks, can we?"

This made mama's hands drop and she took a subtle step closer to Rolly. She kept a wary eye on Cal's gun, not even noticing that Rolly was inching toward her as well.

"Heard ya married him," Cal spat. "How could ya do that to me, Linda?" He snatched a bag from his colleague and shouted some orders to the others about remaining still as they back out of the bank.

"There has to be something better than this, Cal," mama pleaded with him.

It was that optimism, that hope, she passed on to Rolly. It wouldn't let her just watch him leave in his own mess. Not as scared and pathetic as he was.

She should've let him leave.

the end

"We had something better than this!" he shouted at her, advancing again, despite the protests of the rest of his crew. His gun was waving more frantically than before, making mama step back. "We had it, and you smashed it to pieces! We could've had so much more than this pitiful bank could even dream of—do you understand that? Then you had to....you...you...."

His voice trailed in desperate, but shallow, anguish. His gun rose a little higher, and his trigger finger shook just enough.

Rolly admitted once that it wasn't the sound of the gun firing that scared him, it was Calvin's raised voice. It was the shouting he had become far too familiar with to trust the aftermath would be anything but harmful. He could never stop Cal from hitting mama. He knew that. He could never stop him from shouting at her and throwing her on the kitchen floor. He just accepted that mama's house wasn't safe when Calvin was there after bedtime.

But this naive eight year-old boy thought he could stop this.

His toy pistol provided him the training and experience to know that when you lift the barrel just right at your target, that was when you were ready to shoot. It took a lift of just a couple of centimeters for Rolly's instincts to kick in.

And the little hero jumped.

He jumped in front of the princess and stopped the bullet from hurting her. He couldn't stop a fist, but he could block a little

the end

bullet.

He knew he could.

And, to his credit, he did.

The idiot did it.

The robbers fled, even Calvin. Before the cops and ambulance got there, the man with the hat Rolly thought he recognized was also gone. Police later found a body near the river that matched Calvin's description. Multiple bullets shot into him, with his own shooting hand detached from his body.

Rolly swears it was O'Shea's doing and that he was the man in the bank with the hat. I have my doubts. It could've been one of his boys; I think mama would've recognized O'Shea himself. Papa denied it all, insisting that Cal probably brought that fate on himself and that we should all forget about it.

But Rolly's shooter was hard to forget. Just like the battle wounds he caused.

Mama sat in the hospital with Rolly, not even going home for food or rest. Papa tried to get her to go home and sleep while he watched him, but she wouldn't budge. She refused to leave her baby's side. The pain and blood loss put the boy to sleep, and he slept for days. Mama cried and watched, watched and cried. Begging him to wake up, mama held his hand the entire time.

The doctor told papa that the bullet damaged some of Rolly's

the end

intestines, but they would probably heal after some time. His spine, however, wouldn't. Mama's tears fell even harder when she heard little energetic Rolly would never walk again. When he woke up, she didn't want to tell him.

So she let him smile and recount the story to papa with pride. He couldn't understand why mama was standing back and quietly sobbing. Papa didn't mind; he always handled the hard truths. He explained it to Rolly. He told him he'd get the best wheelchair money could buy, and that there were plenty of things he could still do for fun without his legs.

Rolly still couldn't understand why mama was crying.

"Mama, I'm alive, though," he told her. He then looked at papa and said in a soft voice, "She'll be okay; mama's tough as nails."

"Hm, tougher, I think," papa agreed, beckoning mama to the bed.

"I'm so sorry, sweetheart," she choked. Mama sat down beside Rolly, holding papa's hand in her lap. "No more baseball."

She didn't know why that mattered so much to her, but Rolly's grin when he'd pass a ball or swing and miss a pitch was always one of the things that kept mama going. But now she had so much more to keep her going. And Rolly couldn't understand why mama couldn't move forward, just because he got a *little hurt*, as he said.

the end

"I'm sorry," she said again, stroking his face.

"No, I had to save you, mama," he grabbed her hand to stop her. "It's what real princes do." Mama sniffled a breathy laugh, and papa smiled proudly. "Now I can just watch the ball games with you in the stands, so someone can explain the game to you. Besides, I was never very good anyway."

Papa laughed, and mama even cracked another deep smile. Lightly ruffling Rolly's hair and papa leaned in close to whisper,

"I told you so, Rolland. I knew you were the hero."

the end

hazel's epilogue

hazel's epilogue

*I can't lie, tears are most definitely streaming down my face. I even
release a sob or two. I knew Grandpa Rolly was in a wheelchair for years,
but I always assumed it was a war injury or something. It turns out, he'd
never had the chance to serve, given his condition. I only assumed because
most old men his age are veterans. Regardless, I could have never guessed
that little eight year-old Rolly could've sustained such a serious injury that
would render him chair-bound.*

My heart is broken.

And that last line.

I knew you were the hero.

Grandpa Rolly was the hero all along.

*Aunt Hazel isn't letting me cry for long. Almost instantly after
wiping her own tears, she straightens her back and grins widely.* "You'd
never meet a happier cripple," *she says.* "The boy in the wheelchair with high
spirits and a killer sense of humor is the Rolly I grew up with—popping
wheelies in parking lots, and giving me rides down the street until I got too
big to fit on his lap."

"When did mama die?" *I ask, afraid to know the answer.*

"Oh, she was only fifty-six. Severe acute pancreatitis, they said.
Nowadays she would've been diagnosed with lupus, too—doctors couldn't tell
if it was the lupus or the excessive amounts of cortisone that damaged the
pancreas, but it doesn't really matter now. Back then, they thought it was
just arthritis and stress so cortisone was her best chance. We've come a long

way, I think."

"What about papa?"

Hazel's face falls. "He held strong for mama. But he didn't last much longer after she passed. Three miserable years without her...his health failed quickly and he made the rest of us just as miserable as he was. Mama really kept him together—you just wouldn't have known it until you saw him without her."

"He got to see you get married, though, didn't he?"

She smiles a little bit. "They both did."

"When was that?"

"1958," her tears start to well again. "Drew was a dream, he was. Only married two years before the war took him from me. I tried to end it all...the day I got the news."

"But Grandpa stopped you," I finish for her. This story, I've heard before. When my eldest sister was diagnosed with severe depression and had to be committed for a few days for treatment, Grandpa Rolly came over and told everyone it would get better, but not quickly. Then he told us of our great Aunt Hazel.

"Rolly stopped me," she repeats. The tears get bigger and she chokes on her words, "The bedtime prince saved me, just like he saved mama. He gave me a reason to stick around. He gave me my deep smile. Mama gave me a hug. Papa gave me a home. They're my story."

hazel's epilogue

*   *   *   *   *

Aunt Hazel died four months after I finished this transcription. We buried her next to Uncle Drew, right across from her mama and papa, on the other side of the bedtime prince and my Grandma Mimi. With some help from Juliet and my parents, her story is being written.

The bedtime prince will live on.

And so will Hazel, Linda, and Russell Bellamy.

Whether Aunt Hazel felt like she had a part in it or not, this story is hers, and it was the happiest time of her life.

Signed,

Keira Sawyer, Journalist

about the author

Renée Tamsin was raised in various parts of the Southern and Midwestern U.S. The one constant in her ever-changing environment was her stories. When not writing tales of adventure and intrigue, she's busy reading them. Renée published her debut series *The Arkis Tales* in 2018, and continues to release installments of the fantasy saga, while working on projects such as *the bedtime prince* on the side

the bedtime prince, her personal ode to family history, is the first of her serial novel publications initially released on Patreon

Like what you've read so far? Support Renée by leaving reviews and sharing her stories with friends and family.